FALL INTO LOVE

by

Elizabeth Suit

Books by Elizabeth Suit

Stella's Diner

Fall Into Love

Dedication

For those whose love language is sarcasm.

CHAPTER ONE
Allison

MOORE THAN WORDS Advertising and Website Design is hopping today. Which means that I, Allison Moore, sole owner and operator am putting the finishing touches on a website update while trying to keep my eyes from crossing. Thankfully, I've been catching all the typos today in between the numerous phone calls requiring my attention. I'm about to scream when the phone starts to ring again, but then I see my favorite client's number come up on the caller ID. Grant was one of my first clients when I went out on my own. We've been together so long that now our relationship has moved way past professionalism, and we flirt constantly. It's fun and light-hearted, and it brightens my day.

"Hey, handsome," I greet, propping my feet up on my desk. He laughs at my casual greeting.

"Hey, cutie. How are you today?"

"Good. Just finished your updates."

"Terrific! I have something new for you. I got in the first samples of my protein shake, and we'll need to add them to the online store with the description."

"You seriously are telling me this now after I have everything spaced out correctly? I am *so* charging you extra!"

"I'm sorry, but I wasn't sure if they were going to work out and didn't want to hold up the other stuff."

In my best Dr. Evil voice I respond, "My new hourly rate is one million dollars. I assume *the* trainer to the stars can afford it?"

"What would I do without your East Coast sass?"

"Be bored?" I quip.

"Probably," he admits.

"Or have more time for your models?"

"That hurts. Especially today." Grant's voice suddenly falls from light and flirty to low and dejected.

"What? Why? What's going on? You actually sound serious for a change."

"Jordan dumped me," he says.

"No way, I thought you guys were getting pretty serious."

"Yeah, I wanted her to be the one, but we had different goals and couldn't make it work. She's off to Canada to work on some movie."

"I'm sorry, Grant. I know you really liked her."

"Thanks. I'll get over it…eventually." His tone somber. "Maybe sooner if you'd agree to be my girlfriend," he says in a more chipper voice.

"First, I refuse to be your rebound. Second, I'm never dating a bodybuilder because I love food too much and couldn't stand the diet you keep. And three, there's this teeny tiny issue that you live across the country."

"I'd move for you." I laugh because I know he's only joking. We both love our jobs too much to ever move for love. We've discussed this during one of our many late-night conversations that we've had as we've become long-distance friends.

"Ha, we've never even Zoomed, how do you know I'm not a troll with a big wart on my nose?" I ask sarcastically.

"I can tell. You don't have a troll's voice. You know, for someone who works on websites, I'm surprised by your lack of social media accounts." He tosses the sarcasm right back and our conversation continues in lighthearted banter.

"All that my clients need to know is that I can do my job. And look who's talking. You don't have your picture up either. I keep telling you, you need to add it so clients don't think you're some creeper dude."

"My celebrities are keeping me busy enough, so no need."

"Are you ever going to give me your stage name?" I ask.

"No way! When you fall in love with me, I want to know it's not just for my body."

"Fine," I huff. I've tried to google him every which way and have found a few bodybuilders with the last name Hudson, but he says he's only under his stage name. *I wonder if I could employ the CIA to figure out what it is?* Based on his voice, he seriously has to be hot.

"Hey, listen, I've got a client coming in so I gotta go, but I'm going to send you some samples, and I'll get the info over to you to do the updates."

"Okay, sounds good."

"Bye, Allison."

I love having a client I don't always have to be professional with. Being my own boss makes my daytime hours a little lonely, and it helps break up the monotony of my day being able to laugh and joke around with someone. Speaking of being professional, after getting off that call, I need to get back to work. So, I dive into the website design for a new law firm.

At the end of my self-imposed workday, I stretch the stiffness away before rising from the desk in my home office. Picking up my phone, I call my bestie to see if she wants to grab some coffee.

"Hey, Morgan."

"Hey, Hooker. What's up?" By the greeting, I can tell she's already left her office.

"Heading for coffee, you going to meet me at Joe's?"

I ask.

"Hell yeah! I'm about to fall over, and I don't feel like nursing a hangover tomorrow," she responds.

"Great! I'll see you there," I say to her as I am heading out the door.

Joe's is on the corner between our apartments. The light-blue brick building with a pink canopy featuring a steaming "cup of Joe" is a beacon to the weary at the end of a long day. The scuffed wood floors and gleaming white wood paneling give it a farmhouse vibe. Morgan and I have been friends since high school but lost touch when we went away to different colleges. We reconnected at Joe's one day and were shocked that we ended up living so close to each other.

The euphoric scents of coffee and baked goods surround me as I walk in the door of the quaint coffee shop. Even with its small size, it's split into three sections. The back is for the techies desperate for an outlet to complement their high-octane buzz. The living room is where Lululemon moms moan about their kids. And the front section is for people watching. Mini fresh flower bouquets sit on the tables lining the large windows that look out onto the busy street. When our regular barista, Katelyn, sees me walk in, she nods her head in greeting. I hold up two fingers letting her know Morgan will be joining me. While I'm waiting at the pickup counter, Morgan strides in wearing a sleek black suit with a short, but respectable-length skirt. She is stunning with her olive skin, white-blonde hair, and stick-thin figure. A stark contrast to my auburn hair, creamy complexion, and slightly curvier figure.

"So, what's up?" Morgan asks as we take a seat at our usual table in the corner by the front window. "When you call me to meet at Joe's, I know you need to talk about something."

"I talked to Grant again today. He needs more updates. He's starting to sell some new protein shake."

"Oh, your cross-country phone crush. I see from your cheesy grin that things are going well with him." Morgan raises a brow while taking a sip of her mocha latte.

"It's always good to chat with Grant. Today was hectic, so it was nice to hear his voice." I grin and take a sip of my caramel creme.

"You think you two will ever meet in person?" she asks.

"I doubt it. I don't plan on flying to the West Coast anytime soon for someone I'm not dating, and he's not planning on leaving his lucrative business to come here." I readjust in my seat and sit back. "Although he did say he'd move here for me. I'm sure he was just flirting. He just broke up with a model for goodness' sake, and I'm no model."

"And you just broke up with a controlling asshole

who only wanted you for your looks, so don't think yourself less than beautiful and worthy of such attention."

I roll my eyes. "This is just fun and light with no expectations. It's nice to have a guy friend to talk to."

"That's great but now we need to find you someone local to, ya know, relight the flame. Maybe you'll find someone this weekend at the pub crawl." She nudges me with her elbow, an evil sparkle in her eye.

"Maybe. It would be nice," I sigh wistfully and stare out the window at the street wondering if Mr. Right is passing by as we speak.

"No maybes, we both need to get laid. It's been like a month for me, and how long for you?"

"A month?" I gasp. "How do you even live? Like, oh my God, are you sure you haven't shriveled up down there?" I redirect, clutching my chest for dramatic affect.

"Funny. But seriously, we need to find some men. Random hookups are fine, but I'd like more," she says.

"Whoa, whoa, whoa. You, Miss I-never-sleep-with-the-same-guy-twice, want more? You, the one who told me I was getting too serious, too soon with Roger—"

"Roger was a douche. No one should end up with Roger."

"Fine. So, what's your plan?" I ask.

"Plan? It's like you don't know me at all. I'll just keep bar-crawling until I find the right one. Speaking of which, did you get the new shirts for Saturday's crawl?"

"Yeah, I just got them this morning. Nico did a great job this time, and all the words were even spelled correctly."

"Oh, good, because even in my drunken state it was embarrassing to wear a shirt that said, 'The Purple Nipple Crew'," Morgan admits.

I crack up at the memory. We both got a lot of numbers on our shirts that night. I sober and start filling her in on the crawl details. "We have about five bars on the list. I decided to stay on Carroll Street this time to make it easier for everyone."

"Oh my God, do you remember her? She was hilarious. Dancing around, giving everyone beads when it wasn't even Mardi Gras," Morgan says.

"Yes, that's why I call it Carroll Street in her honor."

"That's perfect. I think I'm going to head out. I need to get out of these clothes." We stand and gather our trash.

"Oh, I almost forgot to tell you. Mrs. G is moving out. Her son is moving her to a care facility after she almost broke her hip last month. Any chance you want to move across the hall from me?" I say in a pleading voice. "We'd have so much fun!"

"I don't think I can get out of my lease for at least a few more months, so it probably won't work out timing-wise," she says disappointed.

"Aw, bummer." I pout. "Okay, I'll see you Saturday."

We hug and walk to the door. I'm not paying attention and try to *pull* the *push* door when the door gives, I fall forward and smack my nose into an incredibly defined chest which then causes me to flop down, hard, on my butt.

I look up startled. Morgan is at my side trying to help me up when large hands scoop me up from the other side and right me back on my feet.

"Whoa, be careful there." Big brown eyes stare into my soul as strong arms steady me. He almost glows as if he's an angel sent to earth to pick me up at this very moment.

"Thank…Your…Eyes…Arms." *Am I making any sense? Stars are swimming above my head right now.* I shake my head and groan, touching my face. When I pull my hand away, I see blood. *Is my nose actually broken?* I hear a soft chuckle and it brings me out of my daze.

"Do you think it's broken?" The man of my dreams says softly while cradling my face with his hands, checking me over.

I pull back and look to Morgan to help me form coherent words. Because there is pain, gorgeousness, and blood, and I am too stunned to speak.

"Let me get you a napkin, Ally." Morgan returns to

my side and is wiping my face before I can register that she left. "Should we go to the hospital?" she asks.

"I-I don't think so." I look between the two of them still in a daze.

"I am so sorry. Please, let me walk you home. Make sure you're all right." His face contorts with genuine concern.

"But I don't know you. I'm not supposed to go home with strangers." My bottom lip is trembling, and my eyes are watering from the embarrassment of falling. *What am I, five?*

"I'll take her home. Thank you for helping," Morgan offers for me as I nearly trip over my own feet.

"I'm glad I could help. Feel better, Ally." Big Brown Eyes moves aside and holds the door open for us.

"I'm going to marry that man," I whisper. Morgan chuckles and helps me back to my apartment.

CHAPTER TWO
Oliver

I'M SITTING AT the breakfast bar in my modern, barely used kitchen finishing my morning toast when I get a call from my agent. *Can't this man take a day off? It's Saturday for goodness' sake.* As Frank starts droning on with my latest crime novel release figures, my mind drifts to the girl, Ally, from the coffee shop. She didn't introduce herself, but I heard her friend say her name as we looked her over. She was so cute with that dazed look on her face. I wanted to walk her home to make sure she was okay since she wasn't making any sense, but it looked like her friend wanted to take care of her. I didn't want to come across as a stalker, so I stepped aside. I could kick myself for not getting her number, but it didn't seem like the right time for introductions. I can't believe that having practically lived at Joe's since I moved to the city I haven't seen her before. Maybe it's because I usually stay in the back with the rest of the techies typing away on my latest novel.

"Sales are looking great as always," Frank says.

"Good, let's keep it that way. It was a long time coming, and I want to stay where I am," I respond, coming back to the present and focusing on the conversation.

"I like you on top."

"Frank! I don't think it's wise for us to have that type of relationship," I jest.

"I meant on top of the sales charts," he corrects.

"I'm glad you cleared that up," I continue to tease him, knowing my straitlaced agent is now all flustered.

"Now, what's up next for you?" he says, changing the subject.

"I just wrapped up my current manuscript and sent it to the editor and am mapping out the next one in the series. Since we have a buffer, I'll probably take a mini break this weekend and read for fun, then get back to it."

"Great. We can't get behind."

"I'm aware. And you know that pressuring me makes my brain seize up and no words enter of any kind."

"I know, I just like to know where you are on your schedule so I can keep my own on track. Have a good weekend, and I'll bug you again in a few weeks."

"Looking forward to it," I deadpan and disconnect.

Frank is a good agent but I'm also a good client who doesn't need a lot of handholding. I know my schedule and how many words I have to knock out each day to make it happen.

In an effort to make the most of this weekend, I pull up the schedule for Finnegan's and notice that my favorite acoustic guitar duo will be playing tonight. Since I have plenty of time before then, I decide to take a quick trip out of the city to visit my mom.

"Mom?" I CALL as I enter my childhood home without knocking. The smell of home-cooked meals and Mom's gardenia perfume has settled into its bones and brings back memories of my happy childhood as I inhale the scents. All the oversized, bulky furniture, complete with Dad's blue Lazy-Boy chair, are still in the same position. Vacuum marks on the plush tan carpet confirm that Mom still does her nightly ritual of vacuuming before bed to keep everything clean and tidy.

"Oliver? Is that you?" I hear from some far corner of the house.

"Where are you?" I ask.

"Basement! Come down and see this." I set the lilies I brought her on the kitchen counter and walk down the steps.

"What are you doing down here?" I ask as I step off the last step into the finished club basement.

"I'm putting a shower in the bathroom."

"What? By yourself?" I ask aghast as I meet her at the bathroom door.

"Sure, why not?"

"Why not? Because taking a few classes at Home Depot does not make you a certified plumber."

"Ha ha, Mr. Funnypants. I had Tom run the pipes, I just need to put in the stall and then retile the floor. Easy peasy. Actually, while you're here, help me line it up to the pipes he installed." I do as I'm told. "There, that's perfect, now I can just seal it all up and do the floor and be all set. Maybe I'll repaint. What do you think?"

"I think that I don't know why you are doing all this."

"In case I have guests," Mom explains as her eyes roam the walls and ceiling. I can tell the wheels are spinning in her head trying to decide on a color.

"How many guests do you expect when you have a full bath upstairs they can use?"

"You never know. Family, friends…in-laws…grandchildren. A mother needs to be prepared for anything." She twirls her hands in the air as she lists the possibilities.

"Mother."

She holds onto my shoulder as she looks me in the eye.

"Oliver. Honestly, how have you not met a nice girl living in that big city?"

"Maybe because I live the life of a reclusive writer?" I shrug.

"Oh, how I wish your brother were here to get you out more. I need grandbabies to spoil."

"Do you give Ty the same amount of flack?" I ask folding my arms across my chest.

"Of course, I do. You know your father and I loved you both evenly, so therefore, I nag evenly." She hugs me. "But seriously, make sure you get out and have fun and experience life a bit. You never know when you'll run into a nice girl to bring home."

"Well, I am going to a bar tonight."

"Ah, perfect. Make sure to bring me back a daughter-in-law."

"I'll do my best, Mom."

If my mom was as worried about her own propensity for disaster as much as she was about me finding her a daughter-in-law, I wouldn't have to worry about turning gray early. I love my mom, I do, but if the misshapen shrubs and crooked pole of the mailbox in front of the house are any proof of her inability to complete home repairs, that is just the beginning, and I'm crossing my fingers that bathroom remodeling is where she actually excels.

"Good. Now, follow me upstairs so I can feed you before you go."

"Yes, ma'am." I follow Mom upstairs and sit at the

kitchen table while she puts her flowers in a vase and starts fixing grilled cheese sandwiches and tomato soup for the two of us. I tell her about my new release, and she tells me about her friends and the other updates she's done to the house. I'm so thankful to hear she is happy and keeping busy since we lost my dad a few years ago from a sudden heart attack.

We were all pretty lost for a while without him, and Ty decided to get as far away from the memories as possible by fleeing to California. But now we've all settled into our new lives, and I think he'd be proud of us.

After lunch, I head back to the city with some extra leftovers she had in her fridge to eat for dinner. I stop and grab a new notebook for plotting my next book and then get ready to go to Finnegan's.

CHAPTER THREE

Allison

I T'S FINALLY THE night of our monthly bar crawl. It's a chance for the gang to get together and blow off steam all while raising money for charity. I carefully apply makeup around my sore, badly bruised nose before heading out. Thankfully it isn't broken and is only slightly swollen, but I could do without the purple and yellow coloring that is setting in.

We are pre-gaming at Carlos and Adriana's. There are eight ladies adorned in hot pink T-shirts with Bardacious Babes written on the front, and a graphic of a big-chested woman with a messy bun on top of her head holding a shot glass on the back. Carlos and Adriana round off our group of ten bar crawlers. Both are in the same hot pink, but his shirt says 'Hers', and her shirt says 'His' on the front with Pub Crawlers Anonymous, the official name of our group, on the back. We get a new shirt every month for our crawls thanks to Carlos's friend Nico.

Carlos stops the music to get everyone's attention. He's our shepherd for the night. He makes sure we are safe and that we get to each bar so no one accidentally gets left behind once our drunken stupors take over. He's not a big drinker, so he's happy to do it. Adriana used to be in charge until they met at one of the bars on a hop and they've been attached at the hip ever since. Now the rest of our group is hopeful we'll find our Carlos one of these nights and then live happily ever after.

"Okay, ladies. Let's go find your men!" Carlos cheers. We all woot and holler back. Then he looks at Adriana and they burst out laughing. "Sorry, everyone, I didn't mean to sound like a pimp." His cheeks are turning bright red. "Uh, let's just go get our drink on!" he corrects, and we all hustle out of their apartment still cheering at the prospects for a great night.

We're at the third bar and I'm shimmying to the beat of the alt-rock music when strong hands grab my waist from behind. I spin around with my hand raised ready to slap the person silly when I'm throttled by piercing dark eyes taking in every inch of me, and I'm suddenly not so upset about it.

"Excuse me sir, but those are my hips you're holding on to there," I sass.

"Oh, pardon me, I thought they were mine," he banters back in a thick Latin accent and holds his hands up.

"You thought these curvy hips were yours, huh? Maybe you should try again to make sure you know the difference in the future." I shimmy and suddenly one of his legs is in between mine moving in perfect rhythm.

"Lemme see." He slowly slides his hands around my waist and rubs down to my ass and back up to my hips."

"Whoa there, I said hips." He looks worried for a moment, but his face relaxes when I smile, hold his hands in place, then reach around and grab his ass.

"You're a little forward, don't you think?" He smarts back.

"Me? You started it. You get what you give," I say, leaning back my torso while keeping my hands in place.

"Is that so?" he says.

"Yes, that's so." I give his butt a good squeeze and step back. "I'm Allison, nice to meet you," I say, holding out my hand.

"Daveed," he says, taking my hand and kissing the back of it. *Where did this guy come from?* "Care to have a drink with me at the bar?" he asks, but is already leading me off the dance floor. I look to Morgan, and she nods that she'll keep an eye out for me. I also notice that Carlos and Adriana are cuddled up at the end of the bar and are keeping tabs on all of us as well.

"So, what's with all the pink shirts?" He starts, raising his hand to the bartender for service.

"Monthly bar crawl with my friends. Each month we

pick a charity to donate to, and this time it's breast cancer awareness, hence the pink." I say, waving my hand down the front of my shirt.

"Very nice. So how many of you are in this group?"

"Ten all together."

"Wow, you have a lot of friends."

"I do. And we all look out for one another, so you better watch yourself, mister!" I poke his chest.

"Yes, ma'am," he affirms in his deep, rich tone. "Mind if I join your group for the night? I'd hate to see you run off to the next bar without me. And I love to dance."

"We have two more to go, and sure, the more the merrier. Especially if you have testosterone. The only guy is Carlos, and he's spoken for." I nod toward the lovebirds at the end of the bar. Daveed chuckles.

"How'd you all come together?" The bartender finally comes over and we order two beers before I answer.

"Morgan is my best friend from high school, who I reconnected with after college, and Adriana and the rest of the girls are a mix of sorority sisters from college. We were all in different sororities but ended up here in the same area so we've kinda started our own little group. So, what about you? Tell me about yourself." He takes a sip of the beer that was just set in front of us before proceeding.

"I was raised in Argentina, and now I'm a dance

instructor here in the city."

"Ah, a dance instructor, now I know why you're so handsy," I tease.

"When I see a beautiful figure with moves such as yours, it's hard to resist."

"So, is that how you meet women, usually? You just go up and grab them?"

"No, I think I'd be arrested by now." He chuckles.

"Maybe you should be. Why me?"

"I could feel your sensualness. I felt a kindred spirit within you. Your body called to me."

"My body called to you, huh? Does that line work on everyone?" I take a sip of beer and lean against the bar trying to gauge if he's for real or a player. I figure it's time to move on from Roger the douche and give him a shot.

Carlos beckons me over, and I grab Daveed's hand to bring him with me.

"Is it time to move to the next bar?" I ask, looking at my watch.

"Yep, let's round them up," Carlos says.

"Daveed, it's time to jump in the deep end. We're on to bar four and have to round up seven tipsy, horny women. You ready?"

"Let's do it!" he cheers, and I pull him toward the dance floor to find the rest of the girls.

After I find the last one in the ladies' room, we're off

to the next bar. The heavy metal music is thumping when we arrive, and we grab drinks then start head-banging with the beat. I don't go full throttle but join the best I can. The girls are all over Daveed and I have to say I'm getting slightly jealous. I mean, he's tall, dark, and sexy, what more could you want? Every once in a while, he looks over at me and his eyes seem to say, help me.

I finally drag him out to the back patio for some fresh air.

"You're not kidding, those women are horny. I think my butt's a little sore from the grabbing." He rubs his backside before we take a seat at one of the tables.

"Yeah, I should have warned you, but you look like you could take care of yourself."

"Of course, but I wanted to spend more time with you," he laces his fingers through mine.

"Do you happen to know seven guy friends we can pawn them off on?"

"I'll see what I can do. I have a few at least. So, where do we go next?" he asks, stroking my hand with his thumb.

"We always end at Finnegan's. It's our favorite."

"This is a lot of fun. Thank you for agreeing to let me join. I'm sorry if I gave you the wrong impression." He leans in as if to kiss my cheek.

"Allison, Daveed, let's go," Carlos calls to us, interrupting Daveed. He pulls back and we drop hands as we stand.

"To be continued," I tease as we follow the group out of the bar and to Finnegan's. Daveed takes my hand back into his as we walk down the sidewalk. It is warm and strong. I squeeze his hand, and he smiles down at me and gives me a wink. I smile back and float into the bar.

I decide I'm done dancing for the night. Finnegan's is a quaint pub with live music by local artists. The dim light and dark, wood-paneled walls make it the perfect place to slow down after a night of dancing. Some girls don't prefer the mellow atmosphere and return to their favorite bars from the crawl and others go home early. Tonight, I want to get to know Daveed and exactly how our bodies talked to one another. And how they could be talking to each other in the future.

I lead him to a corner booth, where it's quieter and darker, and let him know I'll be right back with drinks.

"I need two beers, please," I yell to Luke, our hunky bartender whose boyfriend is the luckiest man on the planet.

"You got it, A!" he yells back.

"Ally?" I hear from a guy to my right. I look over and see it's the guy I ran into at Joe's. "Hey! How's your nose?" he asks.

"Oh, hi." I pause, because I don't remember giving him my name, and I know he didn't give me his.

"Oliver," he supplies and holds his hand out for me to shake. "I didn't mean to startle you. I heard your friend say your name." I take a minute to take in his features again and realize they are just as I remembered. Deep brown hair, amber-brown eyes, and a square jaw. He reminds me of Stephen Amell from *The Arrow*.

"Oh. Right. I'm doing just fine. Just a little bruising and soreness." I gently touch the side of my nose. "I've still managed to dance the night away. Thanks for asking."

"You're welcome. You come here a lot?"

"Yeah, Morgan and I are regulars, so Luke is quite familiar with us, aren't ya?" I ask, looking at Luke as he hands me the beers.

"I sure am. Watch out for this one. She's a handful," Luke informs Oliver.

"Is that so?" Oliver smirks. Luke nods and moves on to the next customer, and Oliver turns and gives me a side-eye with the smirk.

"What?"

"I thought running into you twice was good karmic energy, but now I'm a little worried."

"Oh, you should be," I sass back. Oliver huffs out a laugh and then looks down at the bar. I notice there's a newspaper sitting in front of him. "Are you reading the newspaper...in a bar?" *I didn't even think they printed those anymore.* "Don't you know you should be drinking and enjoying yourself? Meeting new people?"

"Well, I have a beer." He holds up his beer. "I'm enjoying reading the newspaper." He nods and shakes the paper in his hands while letting out a satisfied sigh. "And I've met you and Luke, so it seems that I am, in fact, meeting new people." I roll my eyes.

"That's not what I meant."

"What did you mean then?" He sets down the paper and leans his arms on the bar.

"I don't know." I wave my hands around in frustration. "You should be moving around, mingling, dancing, talking to people." He swivels on his stool.

"I'm talking to you, and I just moved around. Happy?" He smirks and winks this time.

"Ugh, you are so frustrating. That's not what I'm getting at, at all." I throw my hands up in the air. I don't know what to do with this guy. And why I even care. It's probably those stupid honey-brown eyes making me all gooey inside.

"Is it the presence of the newspaper that bothers you?" he asks, squinting at me. "Because I've done everything else you said I should be doing. And for that matter, we've only just met and you're being awfully bossy. Are you always this intrusive in other people's lives?"

I huff. "No. You're the one who intruded on mine first." I stomp my foot in defiance.

"How so? As I recall it was *you* who ran into *me*."

I huff again and ignore his question because he's sort of right, but I'm too stubborn to admit it.

"Look, I just meant if you are in a social setting, you shouldn't have your nose stuck in a newspaper, you should be doing…something. And hello, the 2020s called, no one reads newspapers anymore!" I finally spit out because my words are clearly not coming out the way they are supposed to, and I'm now considering if I should even have the beer in front of me. Speaking of beer, I need to get these back to Daveed.

"Well, it seems this newspaper has bothered you so much that it made you converse with me, so I think it might have just done the job it was supposed to."

"And what is that?"

"Entertain me. I have to say, I've never been admonished for reading the newspaper. I happen to like the feel of newsprint in my hands. And if you must know, I was reading the new book releases to see what would be interesting to read this weekend."

"Wow, you have an incredibly wild weekend ahead, don't you?" I snark. *Is he always this pretentious?*

"It depends on what I decide to read, I guess." What I wouldn't do to wipe that smug look off his face.

"Look, I'm sorry if I made you feel bad, but the weekends are for fun and partying," I wiggle my hips.

"I enjoy that as well, but I just finished a big project

at work and reading is how I like to unwind."

"I see. Well, I don't want to keep you. I'm sorry if I overstepped, I'm going to blame it on the booze." I point to my shirt and start to walk away.

"It was good to see you again, Ally." I look over my shoulder.

"It was nice to see you too." I continue toward the booth and Daveed but stop short and turn back to Oliver. "Oh, hey, if you really want to enjoy yourself this weekend, you should grab that new Oliver Hudson book. His mysteries are the best. I can never figure out who did it before it's revealed."

"Hm, I think I've heard of him, you know, us having the same first name and all."

"Oh, yeah!" I say, as if his name has escaped me. He just laughs and shakes his head.

"I'll look him up. Thanks for all the advice this evening."

"You're welcome." I nod and turn back toward Daveed, trying to figure out if that whole conversation actually happened or if I'm drunker than I think.

"Was that a friend of yours?" Daveed asks as I set the beers down on the table.

"Who? That guy at the bar? Uh, no. I actually ran into him the other day at Joe's coffee shop and then here at the bar. I haven't seen him around before, so I'm not sure if he's new to the area or what. Kinda weird."

"Sometimes you are just meant to meet people for a reason. Perhaps it is meant to be for you two, no?"

"I doubt it. He was reading a newspaper in a bar and planned to read all weekend. I don't think that's exactly my type."

"And what's your type?" Daveed asks. I grab his arm and smile shyly.

"I think you have an idea." Daveed smiles and takes a sip of his beer. The Oliver guy and the rest of the crowd fall into the background as Daveed and I settle in closer and get to know one another.

CHAPTER FOUR
Allison

AFTER A RECOVERY day on the couch with a greasy burger, lots of water, and pain relievers yesterday, I'm back at work. I have a home office set up in my second bedroom. It's pink and white with gold accents and decked out with all the latest social media recommended accoutrements.

My phone rings and I answer with, "Moore Than Words, how may I help you?"

"Good morning, cutie."

"Good morning, handsome. How may I help you today?"

"I emailed the specs on the protein shake. I included a photo so you could add it to the store and the offerings tab."

"Okay, I can get started on all that today, but you know you didn't have to call. I would have seen the email."

"I wanted to hear your voice this morning."

"Oh brother, you've been single for forty-eight hours and already hitting on me?"

"Maybe."

"Well, for the record, it's nice to hear your voice as well."

"That's good to know. Have a great day, Allison."

"You too. Bye, Grant."

"Bye."

I GET BACK to work, pulling up Grant's email to get started on the new product description. By the time I'm finished, it's time for lunch. I stand, stretch, and make my way to the kitchen and take out my pre-prepped salad. I add the vinaigrette dressing and sit at my kitchen table. It's just a little two-top I purchased second-hand when I moved in. I play around on my phone and see an ad for that Oliver Hudson book I was talking about the other night at the bar. I had forgotten all about it after my night with Daveed. I quickly download it to my e-reader app and start reading. *The hardcover is also on its way.* I'm an avid reader and feel bad for giving that Oliver guy a hard time about it but come on, there's a time and place for it, and a bar is certainly not the place.

Just as I'm bookmarking my page to get back to work, Morgan calls.

"Hey Ally, sorry I didn't call you yesterday. I spent all day wrapped up in bed. It was glorious."

"Uh, huh. What was his name?"

"Jack. Jake. John? Something that starts with a 'J'."

"I thought you said you were ready for something more serious."

"Ally, it's been a month. A month! I was running out of batteries," she exclaims.

"Oh my gosh, Morgan. I did *not* need to know that." I laugh.

"I can't be on the hunt for something serious if my head is only thinking about getting one thing."

"Whatever you have to tell yourself."

"Enough about me. What happened with you and Daveed?"

"Meh." I sigh.

"Seriously? You two didn't look, meh, Saturday night. What happened?"

"We definitely had chemistry but, I don't know, I just didn't think we clicked intellectually at the last bar. However, he did offer me a free dance lesson, so that's not all bad."

"Really? He clearly likes you."

"I guess," I say.

"Go and see how you feel about him, I mean at least you get an hour with that sexy man's arms around you."

"I knew you were my best friend for a reason. I like the way you think."

"When do you go?" she asks.

"Tomorrow."

"Nice. Look, I gotta run. Talk to you later."

"Okay, bye, Morgan."

"Bye, babe."

We disconnect and I finally get back to work.

WHEN I'M FINISHED for the day, I change into my yoga outfit and roll out my mat in front of the large picture window in my living room. After sitting all day, stretching out all the sore muscles is a perfect way to relax and find my Zen. Forty-five minutes later, I'm all loosey-goosey and feel oh so good. My stomach rumbles and I run to the little market near my apartment to pick up a pre-made meal of roasted chicken and vegetables for dinner.

CHAPTER FIVE

Oliver

B EING A PROFESSIONAL writer means your downtime is short-lived. I took the weekend to relax, and I've been writing out my new outline today. I was stuck on how I wanted to end the book, so I called my brother. He's a terrific sounding board and helps me talk out the plot. He usually doesn't have to say much and then, in no time, I have it figured out. Now that I'm satisfied with my outline, I'm suddenly ravenous and am at the local mom-and-pop market picking up dinner.

The owners, Pat and Rose, have run the store for over twenty years and say that working together is what keeps them together. I'd love to find my Rose. I almost had it once and like the idea of having someone to share my life and successes with. Mom and Ty are great, but I'm looking for more. I walk over to the area where there are some homemade meals, made with love by Rose, and try to decide what I'm in the mood for.

As I'm reaching for the single-serve roasted chicken it

gets pulled away from the other side of the kiosk. I jerk my head up and look over the top.

"Hello there. We seem to run in the same circles," I say to Ally, who's peeking over at me. *Yes, I clearly remember her name, and yes, the heroine in my next book may have the same name.*

"You again. Do you live close by?" she asks.

"Not far."

"I'm surprised I haven't seen you before now. Did you just move in?"

"No, I'm a regular at Joe's and get dinner here most nights. I guess the timing was never right." I smile at the possibility that my Rose is standing right in front of me and that the timing has finally worked in my favor.

"Maybe. I'm not much of a cook, so I'm here most nights," she admits with a shrug.

"I'm sure we'll be running into each other a lot more now," I say. She blushes, and I look away and notice that she's taken the last single-serve dish and start scanning for something new.

"I'm sorry, were you going to get this?" Ally asks with concern, holding up the container.

"Yes, but don't worry, I'll find something else." I wave her off.

"If it were more than one serving, we could have shared. Now I feel bad." She frowns and looks around as if searching for other options.

"Well, we could get a whole chicken and have dinner together," I cheerfully suggest, hoping to alleviate her concern.

"Uh…that's sweet and I appreciate the offer, but I just met you and I'm not comfortable going anywhere with you." She squares her shoulders and backs away from me.

"It's a nice night, not too cold, how about we eat at a picnic table in the park? It's public, lots of people walking by." She rolls her eyes up and bites her lip.

"I guess I could do that," Ally agrees, setting down the container while I grab a small oven roaster from the next section over.

"What were you going to eat with your chicken?" I ask.

"I like their steamed, mixed vegetables."

"Perfect, grab that. I love their mashed potatoes, so I'll grab those."

"Thank you."

"Do you need anything else while we're here?" I ask.

"I'll grab some water since we're not eating at home," she offers.

"While you're in the cooler could you grab me a lemonade?"

"Sure thing." She grabs the drinks and we get in line. After we set everything on the conveyor belt, I let her know I'll pay for everything.

"I've got this."

"Are you sure you don't want half? I mean it's not a date, right?"

"Well, not a pre-planned one, at least," I admit in a jovial tone.

"Oh, so it is a date?" she asks, coyly.

"It can be." She laughs.

"Okay, sure. It can be a date. And the first one I've ever been on in yoga gear and a bun on the top of my head." She pats her head and pushes a loose piece of hair behind her ear.

"You look terrific."

"Do you really want to start this relationship off with a lie?" She sticks out her hip and plants her hand on it. I look her up and down then stroke my chin as if in deep thought.

"Well, you could use a little makeup, but I was trying to be nice," I joke and she swats my arm.

"You're terrible."

"No, I just tell the truth and give compliments when people deserve them, and you look beguiling."

"That's a fancy word."

"Charming and enchanting but often in a deceptive way. That's you. You enchant me with your natural beauty, but I know there is more than just beauty to your charm."

"Wow, thank you. That's very sweet of you."

I pay for the items and take the paper bag then come to a halt. She runs into the back of me.

"Oof," she grunts. "Why'd you stop? Did you forget something?"

"You said relationship." I turn and look at her.

"What? When?"

"Just now, you asked if I wanted to start our relationship on a lie."

"Oh, yeah, so?" She looks puzzled.

"So, you admit we're going to have a relationship," I explain.

"Well, that's what people do, it's a common word. We have relationships with everyone we know. Friends, co-workers, family. Relationship doesn't mean romance."

"Ah…I see…well then, let's see if we can enjoy a meal together and define our relationship. Come on, I have the perfect spot." I lead her out the door and toward the park, grabbing her hand with my free one.

"Dude, I just met you, and you're already asking me to define our relationship?"

"Yep!" I state, pulling her along.

"Well, if you rush me, you might not like the answer, so you better slow down. I'm a city girl, I don't trust so easily," she says, pulling back.

"Gotcha. Hopefully, after we have dinner, you'll see I'm a pretty trustworthy guy."

I drop her hand when we get to my favorite table in

the park, and we take a seat. We're next to a small pond and you can see the city lights twinkle above as if stars in the sky. I look back to Ally and see that she's followed my eyes to the sky. When she returns her gaze to me, she says, "Nice night. I love this fall weather."

"Me too," I agree. "This is my favorite spot. I enjoy people-watching when I get in a writing slump. I like to watch their mannerisms and how they interact with each other. It's helpful when creating characters. For instance, watch that couple." She turns and looks. "See the way he's leaning in?"

"Yeah?"

"They're about to kiss. He's leaning to see if she'll come the rest of the way in." We continue to watch and sure enough, they kiss. We both turn away to give them privacy.

"So the *Hitch* theory works."

"What theory?" I squint my eyes in confusion.

"*Hitch*. The rom-com movie." When I continue my blank stare as no recognition registers, she continues. "Will Smith. Kevin James? Nothing?"

"Will Smith the action star?" I say, and she deflates.

"He also did a rom-com and a very good one at that," she informs me sitting up straight again.

"Sorry. I'm not a big rom-com guy. Action and thriller movies are my genre."

"Ah, gotcha. Well, Alex Hitchens, Hitch, explains to

a character he's helping how to lean in for a kiss before his big date. The guy is supposed to lean in ninety percent and then girl will lean in the other ten, if she wants a kiss." I laugh. "He helps guys get out of their own way to have successful dates."

"Sounds like a fun movie."

"It is, there are some truly funny parts where dates go wrong. You should know that if you stick around, you'll see I tend to talk in movie quotes."

"I can't wait for you to educate me on all the movies I've missed out on," I say as Ally is opening the food containers while I hand her the plastic utensils I grabbed before we left.

"Thanks. This little knife won't be the easiest to use but I'm glad we don't have to pick at a cooked chicken with our fingers." She starts slicing.

"You're welcome. So, you like romantic comedies and crime novels, what else should I know about you?" I take a bite of chicken as she answers.

"Let's see." She weighs her head back and forth. "I have three brothers who are as big as giants who will pummel your ass if you try anything on me." I can't tell if she's joking or not and then she starts laughing and I can't help but join in.

"So, you're also a big jokester."

"Kinda. Sarcasm is my love language, so you might not always get straight answers from me either. So, yes, I have three brothers, but no, they aren't giants, and no, they won't beat you up. But they are protective since I'm the baby of the family. If they didn't beat up Roger, I'm sure they won't beat up you."

"Roger?"

"Let's save him for another time." She waves her hand as if shooing a pest.

"So, you admit there'll be another time?"

"I admit nothing." She laughs again and takes a bite of food. Her laughter is flirty and infectious.

"What do you do for a living?"

"I'm a website designer and also write descriptions for consumable products. If they can sell it, I can describe it."

"Wow, that's a different combo. How did you get into that?"

"I did an internship for this company in college and worked for them for a while after I graduated to gain experience and then went out on my own. Pretty sweet deal since I can work from home."

"Yeah, it's good and bad, working from home. I can work in my pajamas, but it can also be lonely."

"Do you work from home too?" she asks.

"Yeah, I'm a writer." She looks up from her food and blinks at me a couple of times.

"Writer?"

"Yes."

"And your name is Oliver?" She drops her fork.

"Yes."

"Are you THE Oliver Hudson?" A few heads of the joggers passing by turn and look at us when her voice raises at the recognition.

"Ding!"

"Oh my gosh, I'm so embarrassed. I can't believe I recommended your own book to you!" She slaps her forehead with her hand.

"It was actually cute, and quite flattering. It's nice to know you like my books."

"How did I not know it was you? I've seen your picture on the jacket before." She flops her hand back down on the table.

"My hair was longer then? I just cut it to be a little incognito. My friends say it's like Clark Kent and the glasses. I look totally different when my hair is longer."

"Oh my gosh, wait until my friend Morgan finds out she met you and we didn't even know it. We're both big fans."

"Thank you."

"You're welcome. And you are totally coming over and signing my books."

"Did you just invite me to your place?"

"Well, just to sign the books, of course." She clears her throat and wiggles in her seat before taking another bite of chicken.

"Of course." I smile as she blushes. I think she's fangirling, and she hates it.

"So, any brothers? Sisters?" she asks, changing the subject.

"One brother. He owns a company out in California."

"Oh, wow, are you guys close or are you happy he's out there?"

"We're actually very close, and I miss him a lot. I'm hoping he'll make his way back here someday."

"Who's older?"

"He is."

"Who's cuter?"

"Me, of course," I say, puffing up my chest and giving her a cheesy grin. She laughs.

"I don't know. I think I'd have to decide that for myself."

"Next time he comes to visit, we'll have to all get together. You can let me know what you think."

"When is that?" she asks, before popping a piece of broccoli in her mouth.

"I don't know, but I'm sure you and I will still be together."

"Together?"

"Yeah, sure. You said if I stuck around, I'd learn a bunch of movie quotes, so I guess we're stuck with each other." I give her a wink.

"I also said I admit nothing."

"You invited me to your house."

"To sign books."

"Touché."

"Moving on, what do you like to do in your spare time?" Ally asks.

"I love doing anything outdoors. Playing one-on-one at the basketball courts, soccer, and tennis. What about you?"

"Yoga is my exercise of choice. Keeps me from getting stiff after sitting all day."

"Maybe I should try it. Could you teach me? Ya know, when I come over to sign your books?"

"I might be able to do that," she answers coyly and continues to pick at her food.

"I'm counting on it." I pause and take a few bites of my meal. It's such a beautiful evening. A gentle breeze ripples the pond as the sun sets behind Ally, causing her to glow. I have to shield my eyes, look away, and focus on the joggers and dog walkers passing by. I'm contemplating if I should ask her about the guy she was with at the bar when an older couple passes, holding hands, and I take it as a sign to go for it. "How was your date the other night?"

"Is this your roundabout way of asking me if I went home with that guy?" She puts her fork down and crosses her arms in front of her on the table.

"Uh…maybe?" I cringe as I admit she saw right through me.

"It wasn't a date. It was a bar crawl, and he was a guy we picked up along the way. He's giving me a free dance lesson tomorrow."

"Dance lessons, huh? Sounds like he wants a *relationship* with you." I jest.

"I don't know, maybe he does." She shrugs.

"You looked pretty enamored with him."

"Were you watching us?"

"I might've been," I admit. I smirk and wipe it away with my napkin.

"Hmm, you seem to be awfully interested in my affairs."

"Hmm, maybe I'm testing the waters to see if I have a chance," I respond, honestly.

"Let's just say that I'm currently open to all options that present themselves," she admits.

"I see. For what it's worth, I'm having a nice time with you."

"It has been a nice evening," she admits, uncrossing her arms and starting to clean up. "I should head home. Thank you for dinner." She stands and brushes off her lap.

"You're welcome. Hey, do you have a pen on you?"

"No, why?" she asks, sitting back down.

"I wanted to get your number while I have the receipt to write on."

"First, it's the newspapers, and now you want to write my number down? Do you own stock in paper?" I laugh.

"No."

"Just give me your phone," she states, holding out her hand.

I give it to her with the contact screen open. "There, now you can reach me anytime," she says, placing in back into my palm.

"Thank you. And just for the record, sometimes I like to have a backup just in case I lose my phone," I admit, pocketing my phone in my jacket.

"I'm sure it's unnecessary. Look how we keep running into each other."

"True. Here, take the leftovers with you." I put everything back in the bag and hand them to her. "I'll walk you home." I stand and hold out my elbow.

"Thank you, I'd like that." She stands, takes the arm I've offered her, and I escort her back to her apartment.

"Thank you again for dinner," she says giving me a brief hug.

"You're welcome. Have a good night, Ally."

I watch her walk into her building to make sure she's safe then turn and walk toward my conveniently close apartment.

CHAPTER SIX

Allison

"Morning Hooker, it's your daily morning commute call," Morgan chimes into the phone when I answer.

"Perfect timing. I just poured my coffee and my toast is almost ready."

"And let me guess, the honey, PB, and banana are waiting to be added on top?"

"Of course! Ever since I read that book where the main character ate it all the time, I had to try it, and now I'm sort of addicted to it," I defend. Morgan laughs.

"It is good. I just can't do it every morning. Anyway, what's the latest in your world? It's your day." We alternate days on who gets to dish the dirt since her commute isn't very long.

"Well, you won't believe this, but I ran into that Oliver guy again."

"Again? What's that, like three times now?"

"Yep. Crazy right?"

"Totally, so where was he?" When my toast pops out of my Hello Kitty toaster, I plate it and start adding the fixings but stop to finish my story.

"At Rose and Pat's. We played a game of tug-o-war with the last individual meal. I won, so he suggested we have dinner together. We ended up getting a few things and took them to the park. He called it a date and paid for everything."

"Holy crap, why can't I just fall over a guy like that?"

"Technically I fell into him, but get this, are you sitting down?"

"No, you know I'm walking to work, just tell me."

"HE'S *THE* OLIVER HUDSON!" I scream.

"OMG! You suck. I can't believe you're dating the greatest crime novelist of all time!" Morgan screams back. I have to hold the phone away from my ear.

"It was one date," I say, putting the phone back in place.

"What's he like?"

"Very nice, sweet, charming, and definitely doesn't hold anything back."

"That's so awesome. Do you think he'd sign my books for me?" she asks.

"I'm sure he would, I told him he needed to come sign mine, so if that happens, I'll let you know when to come over."

"You better!"

"Of course I will, you're my girl."

"I'm almost at work so I'll let you go," she says.

"Okay, have a good day. I'll call you after my dance lesson."

"Oh shit. I forgot that was today! Damn woman, what are you going to do with all these men?"

"I'm sure I can think of something. You did say I needed to have some fun." I waggle my eyebrows even though she can't see me and laugh.

"I'm sure. Bye."

"Bye Morgan."

I TAKE THE afternoon off and prepare for my lesson with Daveed. I had a great time with Oliver, but I'm keeping my options open and want to look nice. I throw on a red dress that's fitted at the top and flows at the waist so that I can twirl in style. As I walk into the dance studio, I can hear different types of music flowing from the rooms lining the hallway behind the front desk. I approach the receptionist and give her my name. She lets me know Daveed will be with me shortly. I take a seat in the waiting area and the receptionist hands me a small bottle of water to drink while I wait.

I'm tapping my foot to jazz music when Daveed calls my name. It rolls off his tongue like a melody. When I look up, his gorgeous smile and bright eyes take me in. I know we didn't quite hit it off mentally, but I have to say that with the look he just gave me, my girlie bits are getting a little worked up. I rise and follow him to one of the rooms.

"I'm so happy to see you again. Thank you for coming," he says while twirling me into a classroom. There are full-length mirrors on one wall and the wooden floor creaks as we walk to the middle of the room.

"How could I resist a free dance lesson? I've got to keep my moves fresh!" I banter back with a laugh.

"Is that the only reason you came?" he asks, worry furrowing his brow.

"No! That isn't the only reason," I assure him, patting his arm.

"Good." He sighs and relief washes over his face. "Now, where should we begin?" He thinks for a brief second and then claps his hands. "But of course! I shall teach you the tango."

"I'm all yours." I wiggle in excitement.

"Okay, place your arms up like this," he instructs and I follow, holding my arms out to the side. "And I will hold you like this. He matches his hands up with mine. Then you just let me lead. Okay?"

"Lead away," I whisper, mesmerized by his deep voice and dreamy eyes.

"Okay, right foot back. One, two, three, to the side, slide." He looks down at me. "Good, let's do it again." We circle around the room and he continues to add steps.

"Now we will promenade." He turns me so we are cheek to cheek and we continue our slow-quick-quick-slow steps. Once he's done walking me through the steps, he starts the music and we dance around the room. I feel like I'm in Argentina dancing down a sidewalk lined with shops and cafés, transported by the music and the scent of his spicy cologne. My head spins, but I don't falter as he steadies me in his arms. We continue for several songs, just dancing and staring into each other's eyes, until he dips me with a kiss on the lips.

"You are amazing. Most people don't pick this up so quickly," he informs me, setting me upright.

"You're just saying that." I blush.

"Not at all. You're a natural. I'd love to spend more time teaching you other dances." He steps away and grabs us some water.

"I'd love that," I say, taking in deep calming breaths while accepting the bottle of water he offers.

"Shall we schedule another date?" *I know. I know what I told Morgan but this experience was kind of amazing and I think he deserves another chance.*

"Yes. Friday night?" I offer, taking a sip of the cool water.

"I will pick you up at seven."

"Perfect. See you then, Daveed." I try to purr his name but I don't think I manage to make it sound as sexy as when he says mine. He huffs out a laugh before placing a gentle kiss on my forehead.

"Till then." He takes my hand and walks me to the front door of the studio. When I step outside, I chug the rest of the small bottle of water to cool my flushed body and grab a cab.

CHAPTER SEVEN
Allison

I SLEPT LIKE a rock after all the dancing with Daveed yesterday, but the euphoria of the moment is gone as the phone has been ringing non-stop today. I've picked up three new clients and am starting on a website overhaul for an existing one. I stretch and roll my shoulders when my stomach starts to growl. Realizing it's already lunchtime, I remove my glasses and rub my eyes. My stomach grumbles again, and I stand and make my way to the fridge.

I have leftovers from my date with Oliver, but I'm not feeling it. I honestly hate leftovers. They taste like sadness. They're never the same as the first time, and I only eat them out of obligation to not waste food. Growing up with three older brothers we never had many leftovers, so I never learned how to make them taste good. I close the fridge and stare at the pantry items. PB&J on crackers sounds even less stellar so I grab my sneakers and make a trek to the market. Maybe I can find something to add to the leftovers to make them tolerable for dinner.

Since we're having an Indian summer, it's a gloriously warm, sunny day and I decide to stop by the post office before getting lunch to see if I have anything in my post office box.

You know how you have certain thoughts and you think they are a good idea at the time? Yeah, well, going to the post office first might not have been the best idea, as I'm now walking down the street with a box full of sex toys. And, you're probably saying to yourself, what's the big deal, they come in non-descript boxes. I say nay-nay, not when you are doing product ads and they send them for free, apparently. Because I'm walking down the street with a box that has several pictures with certain body parts blacked out and a pretty good view of the items in the box. I. AM. MORTIFIED. I hustle down the street, trying to avoid eye contact with passersby.

Thankfully, Pat and Rose know me and know what I do, so I'm hoping I can get in and out quickly without drawing too much attention to myself. I decide to get a small cart to put the box in while I shop, in hopes of being discreet.

I'm grabbing some items for lunch, something to fix up the leftovers for dinner, and some breakfast.

"Hello again." I don't have to turn to know who is behind me—Oliver.

I slowly turn in hopes of blocking the contents of my cart with my body since he's behind me.

"Oh, hey, hi. How are you today?"

"Great. I had a really nice date the other night, and I've been thinking about her ever since."

"Oh?" I raise one eyebrow.

"Yeah, arguably the coolest girl I've met, and I'm hoping she'll go out with me again."

"I think she'd like that."

"How about Friday night? Seven p.m.?"

"I think she could make it work. What's the dress code?"

"Casual."

"Great. Pick me up at my place?" I ask.

"My pleasure."

"Okay, well, see ya later. Bye!" I start to walk away.

"Wait, can I walk you home?" I stop and turn back.

"Uh, no, I'll be fine on my own," I say, trying to keep the basket shielded with my body.

Oliver peeks over my shoulder.

"Are you sure? You look like you have a good bit in there."

"I assure you; I'll be fine." I try to push the cart in the opposite direction.

"Okay then, see you Friday," he says.

He has a disappointed look on his face as he turns to go. I scrunch up my nose and sag my shoulders in defeat.

He might as well know.

"Wait, okay, fine, but I have to warn you." He stops and turns back to me.

"Warn me?"

"I have something with me and it's kind of embarrassing." I cover my eyes with my hands.

"Come on, it can't be that bad." He peeks into the cart as I move out of the way to let him see the box.

"Bwahahahaa." Oliver doubles over in laughter when he sees it, and I start laughing with him.

"I rescind my acceptance of your offer for dinner on Friday." I playfully push him away.

"Oh no you can't because I have to know why you have that box with you."

"I'm not telling you now." I tease. "As a matter of fact, I'm going to go check out and go home. *Alone*." I turn to push the cart away but Oliver stops me.

"Come on, you can tell me all about it when I walk you home." He's still laughing when I shrug and finally agree.

After Rose checks me out with a grin and a wink, Oliver and I step out onto the sidewalk with me holding the shopping bags and him holding the inappropriately labeled box.

CHAPTER EIGHT

Oliver

AFTER I DROP Ally off with a good chuckle and a better understanding of her job, I get a call from my brother Ty. He doesn't usually call during the day because of his crazy client schedule, so I immediately answer.

"Hey, what's up?"

"I'm coming home!"

"You're coming to visit?" I ask.

"No, not to visit. To live!"

"No way! That's awesome! When?"

"As soon as I can find a place. Can you help?"

"Of course! What are you looking for?" I inquire.

"I need something big enough that I can put in a home gym for clients, and then I can look for a retail space once I get there."

I'm standing outside Ally's door when a woman carrying flyers comes out of the door across the hall.

"Yes, Mr. Genova. I'll send out these flyers and keep

you posted when we have showings. Thank you."

"Hey Ty, let me call you back." I disconnect with Ty and approach the woman. "Excuse me, did you say showings? Is that apartment for sale?"

"Yes, sir. Are you interested?"

"I might be. Could I see it now?"

"Yes. The owner has already moved out so showings are available at any time. Follow me. I'm Shirley Keys." She's a woman in her forties with a medium build, brown hair pulled back in a bun, and kind brown eyes.

"Oliver. Nice to meet you." We shake hands.

She knocks on the door before entering. "Mr. Genova? I just ran into this gentleman in the hallway, and he'd like to look around."

"Terrific," the silver-haired, burly gentleman says. "I'll leave you to do what you do best. Please let me know if you have any questions after you've taken a look. I'm just grabbing the last box of things to take to my mother."

"Thank you," I say, peeking into the doors and out the large picture windows. There's good light and open space for all Ty's equipment.

"Let's start with the bedrooms. We have two bedrooms and two full baths. One is an en suite and the other is for guests," Shirley explains.

The size of this place is impressive for an apartment in New York. I have an idea of what Ty can afford and hope the price is right.

"The kitchen is a decent size, but I think you'll agree that this big open space is worth it," Shirley continues. And I couldn't agree more. Ty will love the area to set up all the weight equipment.

"This is great. My brother is moving here from California. I'll take a flyer and give him the information and get back to you. I can't speak for him, but I like what I see." Mr. Genova nods his head in understanding before heading out the door with the box in his arms.

"All right. Thank you for your interest. Let me get your information," Shirley says.

I share my contact information and tell her I'll be back in touch. The flyer has a website link for Ty to view the online slideshow. We shake hands and I head back to my apartment.

WHEN I RETURN to my place, I send Ty the info. Over Zoom, we look at the website together.

"What do you think?" I ask.

"The open space is amazing. I've been looking online but everything's been so small with more focus on the bedrooms."

"That's what I thought when I saw it. Mine doesn't have that big of an open area. We're pretty lucky we can afford some nice places."

"Yeah, but I'd rather have Dad."

I'm surprised by Ty's comment. After our dad passed, we each got an inheritance that helped us move out and set up our own businesses. He took his to California to avoid the memories, and I stayed close to Mom. I know not to say much more on the subject and continue.

"Me too. Anyway, this place just went on the market, so you might want to scoop it up. Plus, it's only a five-minute walk from my place."

"Let's see if they'll come down in price. That will help with the moving cost. I'll call Shirley when we get off the phone," he says.

"Are you going to tell me how I'm getting you back here?"

"I've been talking to some of my clients, and they want a 'me' in New York when they travel back and forth for work. So, I talked to Ben, and he's going to run the LA location, and I'm going to start one in New York."

"That's so cool. Have you told Mom yet?"

"I wanted to wait until I found a place and surprise her."

"I'll keep it under wraps but, bro, I'm so excited."

"Me too. I love LA but I'll be happy to be able to work on both coasts. It's an exciting opportunity. Hey listen, I'm going to go call this realtor, and then I'll let you know what happens.

"Okay, good luck! Talk soon!"

I disconnect with Ty and get back to my manuscript, but it's hard to focus. Between meeting Ally and the idea of my brother living in the same city again, it has made it hard to think about murder plots. I close my notebook to look up restaurant choices for Friday night but quickly realize I know just the right one. Then I search for backup apartments for Ty.

CHAPTER NINE
Allison

FRIDAY NIGHT DATE night is officially here and I'm just putting the finishing touches on my makeup and dancing to some music when there's knocking at my door. I'm so excited to be going out with Oliver. He's kind and sweet and, hello, a bestselling author. His face and book covers have graced billboards in Times Square! I'd love to pick his brain. You know, writer to writer.

I adjust my navy blouse and smooth my hands down my dark skinny jeans before fluffing up my hair and skipping to the door. I swing it wide open in excitement.

"Hellloooo, Ol-Daveed." I quickly correct myself as Daveed is standing in front of me, and I have no idea why. Until a jolt from my memory explains it to my brain. You made a date with two guys on the same night, you dope. *Shiiiit.*

"Hello, my dear. You look amazing. Are you ready to head out?"

"I, hmm, uh," I stutter and have no idea what I'm

going to say. Daveed is standing there in a gorgeous white linen suit and staring at me like I have two heads when Oliver shows up behind him. My eyes bulge, and instead of wishing I were about to have a very sexy evening with two handsome men, I'm wishing this were a fantasy and I could pop out of this dimension and into a new one.

Daveed and Oliver introduce themselves to each other when I don't speak.

"Oh, hey, you were the guy she was with at the bar the other night, right?" Oliver asks, breaking the silence while I stare and move my mouth like a fish gulping air out of water.

"Yes. Allison and I, how do you say, got close," Daveed explains. It's then that my brain finally receives information in order for me to form words.

"Well, not that close," I blurt. Both men look at me. Daveed with hurt, Oliver with suspicion.

"Did I get the day wrong?" Oliver asks.

"Uh, no. As a matter of fact—and you'll both think this is funny—I have a date with both of you tonight," I explain with a shrug and a sheepish grin that I hope looks cute and not stupid like this very situation. "What if we all caught a movie?" I ask, hoping I don't hurt either one of them.

"Well, I have to say, a threesome isn't my style, so I'll see you around Ally. I'm sure we'll meet up at the market some time. Good evening." Oliver gives us both a curt nod and walks off.

"Oliver!" I call out trying to stop him, but he doesn't look back. Daveed and I watch him until he's out of sight.

"Well, now that it is just you and me..." Daveed holds out his arm for me to take. "Shall we?"

I look at his arm then at the stairs where I last saw Oliver, and my lip quivers. I'm not this girl. I like to have fun, but I'm not a multi-dater. I also know I'm not committed to either of them, and well, Daveed is hot, so if Oliver doesn't want to fight for me then maybe we'll just be friends who meet at the market.

CHAPTER TEN

Oliver

I LITERALLY STOMP back to my apartment like a child. I tried to keep my composure and remain a gentleman, but now I want to hit something. I know Allison isn't mine and we're not even officially dating but seeing her with that guy was like a punch to the gut. I may not be a smooth-stepping dancing machine but I'm not chump change.

I plow through the door and beeline to the fridge to grab a beer, then I plop on the couch and call Ty.

"Hey bro, I haven't heard back from Shirley yet," he says.

"That's not why I'm calling. The girl I was supposed to be going on a date with had other plans."

"What? Wait, is this the girl you keep running into that's 'so cute'?" Ty mimics me in a high-pitched voice.

"I didn't say 'so cute'. I said, 'takes-my-breath-away beautiful'. I'm more eloquent than 'so cute', thank you very much. And yes, that girl."

"What happened?"

"I showed up and there was another guy already there. Some guy she met at a bar."

"No shit?"

"Yeah," I say, pouting to myself.

"I can't believe she picked him over you, man."

"She didn't exactly."

"What do you mean?" he asks.

"I bowed out."

"What? What kind of quitter talk is that? Have I not taught you anything?"

"I'm not getting involved with someone who's just looking for a fling. I've done that."

"Yeah, but it's a lot of fun," Ty practically sings.

"Sometimes," I say.

"Always," Ty corrects.

"Not when you get a stage-five clinger you have no connection with and the vocabulary of a first grader." After my engagement fell through, Ty convinced me to date…a lot. And that's when I found Candy, who talked baby talk and asked me for money. All. The. Time. I thought the baby talk was some cute thing she did to pick up guys, but it never stopped. Just when I thought I was seeing the real her, she'd fall back into that voice, and I couldn't take it. I finally convinced her I wasn't the guy for her and after a few crocodile tears, she left.

"Look dude, do you like the girl?" Ty asks me.

"Yes. We have great conversations. She's sarcastic as hell, and I'm here for it. She writes. She's funny. I love the way she blushes when she's embarrassed. I just thought she was deeper. I thought it was going some-where. You know they say you can't come on too strong or you'll scare them away. I was trying to be suave."

"Suave? Ha. You have to be confident without being a dick. Show them you have a soft side but that you're not a pushover."

"I thought I was," I say with annoyance.

"Well, I guess you'll never know now that you 'bowed out'."

"Look, I put my all into my relationship with Tracy and what do I have to show for it? An ex-fiancé who now lives in France with some prince."

"He's not a prince."

"He might as well be. So being the nice guy doesn't always work, and I'm not about to get into something with someone who apparently has so many men in her life she can't remember which night she scheduled dates with them." I huff out, exasperated, and start pacing.

"Well, then, why don't you go to that bar you were talking about and see what you can find? I know it won't be the same without your wingman but I'll be there soon to help you out."

"I don't know man." I flop back on the couch and take a swig of beer.

"Fine. Don't take my advice. Just sit on your couch and stew then. You let me know if you're going to be a quitter or a fighter. I've got to go but call me later."

"Bye, Ty. I will." I huff and lay all the way down on the couch.

A montage of my brief meetups with Ally plays through my head. The chicken skirmish at Pat and Rose's. The city lights reflecting in her twinkling gaze across the picnic table. The blush on her face when she admitted she had a box of sex toys with her. I still chuckle to myself when I think of the moment she let me see into her shopping cart. I thought she didn't want to be with me and couldn't understand why she had agreed to a date with me if I couldn't even walk her home. When she explained her latest customer acquisition, it took all my willpower not to offer to help her test them out. It always feels so fun and fresh with her. I can clearly see a future with her, and I realize I'm an idiot for not fighting for her.

CHAPTER ELEVEN

Allison

AFTER A NIGHT of dancing and laughing, Daveed walks me back to my apartment.

"Would you like to come up?"

"Oh, yes," he purrs.

I tell him to take a seat on the couch while I grab some wine.

"Do you mind if I use your bathroom? I'd like to freshen up a bit," he says.

"Oh sure, second door on the left," I tell him and pick out my favorite bottle of red wine from the rack on my kitchen counter.

I can't find my bottle opener right away so I'm still rummaging around in the drawers when I hear him come back out into the living room.

"I'll be right there. Just looking for the bottle open-er," I call out.

"Take your time."

I finally find it and open the bottle then grab two

glasses. It will need to breathe a bit, so I have the bottle in one hand and the glasses in the other when I exit the kitchen. What I see next causes everything I'm holding to crash to the floor.

Standing before me is Daveed in all his naked glory. *And hello, it is glorious!* BUT no way is this happening! This is not the way to my heart. Or any other place for that matter.

"What are you doing?!" I screech.

"You asked me for wine. You want me, no?" Daveed asks confidently with his hands on his hips. Dare I say he even swivels them a bit?

"No, no, no, not even a little bit! Get out. Get out. Get out!" I shout motioning him to the door.

In shock, he scrambles to get dressed. While he's zipping his pants, I grab his shoes and shirt and throw them at his chest as I push him out the door.

"But…but…but…"

"No buts. Get out." I push him one last time and slam the door behind me. Resting my back against it, I let out a low growl.

"Bella…"

"Go, Daveed," I say. From the other side of the door, he sighs and walks away.

I've just about calmed my breathing when the door vibrates against my back from a loud knock. In frustration, I swing open the door ready to give Daveed a piece of my mind, assuming he's decided not to give up.

"I said…"

"What?"

Oliver is standing in front of me and I'm dumb-struck for a minute.

"I said…hello Oliver. What are you doing here?" I ask, smoothing my hair and taking another calming breath.

"I just came by to say I'm not bowing out. Date us both, if you want, until I prove to you that I'm the right choice." I blink several times while trying to take in what just happened and what Oliver is saying. I shift my stance while I gather my wits.

"I'll take that into consideration, but I don't think Daveed will be in the picture anymore." Oliver glances over my shoulder and gasps.

"No? Why? What happened?" He sidesteps me and moves to the dark pool of red liquid now soaked deeply into my beige carpet. Then he turns to look me up and down. "Are you hurt?"

"No," I huff and shut the door.

"Okay. Good. You're okay. Good," he repeats, pat-ting my shoulders. "Now, where's the body?"

"What body?" I ask.

"David…Daveed…whatever. You should have kept it here and just rolled him in the carpet. It's ruined anyway." He looks around, for what I have no idea.

"What are you looking for?"

"A trail of blood. I don't see one. Good. You got it cleaned up. Good. Now is there anything he could have left behind that we have to worry about the police finding?" He's looking around, rubbing his chin.

"Police? What are you talking about? This isn't one of your murder books. I spilled the wine!"

"Oh." Without skipping a beat, he whips out his cell phone.

"What are you doing?"

"Goggling how to get red wine out of a carpet. Blood I know, wine I don't."

"Stop. Hold on." I walk toward him into the living room waving my hands. "First you think I'm a murderer, and then you know how to get blood out of a carpet? Why are you even here if you think I'd be capable of such a thing?" He laughs, and now I'm worried he may be a murderer. I slowly walk backward to the door, keeping my eyes on him. He puts his phone back in his pocket and smiles at me.

"I'm just messing with you. I saw the half-naked man running from your apartment. Want to tell me what really happened?" he asks, putting is hands on his hips.

I cross my arms and stomp my foot. "No, I do not. I don't think we're at a point where I need to explain my actions to you."

I'm an independent woman who doesn't need a

man's help. Plus, this guy is confusing the hell out of me. First, he flirts, then he doesn't fight for me. Then he says he's willing to let me decide which guy I want. Then he thinks I'm a murderer. *Hello, can you say emotional whiplash?*

"Fine. I'll just help you clean this up then. The website says, I need a towel to blot and then peroxide and dish soap." And now he's being sweet. I want to stomp my foot again but I refrain, trying to keep the appearance of the mature woman I claim to be.

I uncross my arms, no longer in annoyed defiance, and turn to gather the items. When we're done and I can barely tell where the stain was, I thank him.

"Thank you."

"For helping you or for coming back?"

I squint at his cockiness then relent to the feelings bubbling up inside. "Both," I answer honestly.

He rises from the floor and steps closer. I move in closer and stare at his lips. He places his hands on my waist and pulls me close. I gently lay my hands on his chest, and we stare into each other's eyes. I know I want to kiss him, and I know he wants to kiss me, but I'm not sure if this is the right time. This evening has been one crazy whirlwind from the moment I opened the door to two handsome men. I pull back.

"I better get these things put away. I like to keep things tidy," I blurt out. Oliver steps back and allows me to pass to get around the sofa. When I come back to the living room, he's not where I left him. He's pacing by the door.

"I should go, but are you free for dinner Tuesday?" he asks.

"I would love to go to dinner with you," I say, holding the door open for him.

"I'll pick you up at six?"

"I'll be ready."

"See ya." He lingers in the doorway and looks at my lips then abruptly turns and walks down the steps.

I softly close the door and lean on it. Then bang my head against it in frustration. *Why didn't I kiss him?* I turn, shut off all the lights, then shuffle to my bed and flop onto my fluffy covers, falling asleep in my clothes.

CHAPTER TWELVE
Allison

AFTER I ROLL out of bed in a wrinkled ball of last night's date clothes, I take a quick shower to start the day refreshed. Once I'm washed, dressed, and have had breakfast, I take a second cup of coffee into the living room and call Morgan.

"So then what happened?" Morgan asks.

"We had a laugh, got the stain out, and then…" I trail off thinking of the almost kiss.

"And then…what? Come on woman, spit it out."

"We almost kissed."

"Almost?" she asks.

"I wanted to kiss him. I just couldn't," I relent.

"Why not? Bad breath?" I laugh.

"Bad timing. Daveed got me all flustered, and accidentally scheduling two dates on the same night threw me off," I explain.

"Do you like him?"

"He's sweet and caring, I think I'm falling for him.

Before he left, he asked me out on a real date."

"That's a positive. And I can see why you'd be into him. But can we rewind to the part about him thinking you were a murderer?" I laugh again.

"He was just joking around. I love his sense of humor."

"Joking, huh? Did you look him up yet?"

"Uh, hmm, uh."

"You can stop that right now. Since when don't you google potential guys?"

"Since this one?" I say more like a question. Maybe since I've read every article about the famous author, I feel like I know him and can trust him.

"Oh no, you got it bad girlfriend."

"It's starting to look that way," I admit.

"Let me do it." I hear tapping in the background.

"Wait, don't. I don't want to know."

"You don't want to know if he's a psycho killer?" Morgan asks.

"Nope, I want to live in blissful unawareness."

"Can't let you do that, hold please."

"Morgan, come on, he's a good guy. I know it. I can feel it."

"Then it shouldn't matter if I look him up."

I huff. Why is Morgan suddenly the responsible one when I want to date a hot, interesting guy? She's always been the carefree, date-any-guy one, and I've always been the look-him-up one. Now the tables are turned, and I don't like it. I wanted her to be like she always was.

"What's with you? You usually don't look guys up."

"I know, but there was a guy that was creeping me out the other night and now I'm trying to be like you and be more cautious, and just when I do that, you go off the res." I giggle.

"Oh yikes. I'm glad one of us can be the voice of reason when the other needs it." I tell her.

"Me too. Found him. He was born in New York. Looks like he grew up in the suburbs but moved to the city five years ago. Has a brother and his dad is deceased but his mom is still alive."

"Aw, poor Oliver. I can't even think about not having my dad." I shake my head and hug myself at the thought.

"Right?!"

"So, see, nothing said psycho killer," I reiterate.

"His dad is dead."

"I can't believe you just said that."

"What? I'm just being real here. You don't know this guy at all," Morgan counters.

"I know, but he's hot. And he was a gentleman who walked me home holding a box of sex toys the other day," I defend.

"Wait, what?"

"One new client, plus one incredibly embarrassing

box equaled me running into him at the market. He wouldn't take no for an answer when I told him he didn't need to walk me home, so…he got to carry the box and I got the groceries."

"That's hilarious, one point for Oliver."

"And point two is that he is a famous author. Do you honestly think he'd ruin a good thing by being a murderer?"

"He also writes about characters who conceal their identities." She points out.

"But they always get caught in the end, so I don't think he's a psycho killer!" I raise my voice in exasperation.

"You do realize if he were some random, ugly dude, you'd totally think he was and would be doing your own research right this very minute."

I huff again because she knows me too well, but I don't want to admit what she said is true.

"Fine. Look up how he died."

"Doesn't say. Just that it was sudden. I don't know, Ally, it sounds suspicious."

"Morgan, stop. He's a good guy. I can just tell."

"When you end up dead, don't say I didn't warn you."

"I'll haunt you and only say nice things to you," I assure her.

"You should, since I'm only looking out for you."

"I just want to have fun and not worry all the time. I mean, how many guys are willing to hide a body for you?" I giggle at the memory now that I know he was just joking with me.

"In real life? None. In books? Plenty. And they usually are the murderers! How do you know he was actually joking? Maybe he was feeling you out to see if you could be a psycho-killing duo."

"Very funny. I choose to believe he's a good guy."

"You better let me know where and when the date is," Morgan instructs.

"You're such a Mamma Bear. I gotta run but I'll chat with you later."

"Bye, babe."

"Bye," I say and hang up the phone.

I'm glad I have Morgan in case I ever were to go missing. But there is something so sweet and kind about Oliver that I just can't imagine him being a murderer. Maybe I could find a way to stalk him before our date. Or maybe I've watched one too many rom-com movies. Either way, I grab my laptop, and start googling now that Morgan has put doubt in my head. Too bad most searches don't say things like, 'Roger is not a good option for you' before you go out with them. First stop, a judicial search then down the rabbit hole I go.

CHAPTER THIRTEEN

Oliver

I'M SITTING IN my library feverishly plotting out a revenge sequence that may involve poisoned wine. Thank you, Ally, for the idea. I have several law books open and true crime podcast notes strewn across my desk. I hear ringing in the distance, and it brings me out of my thoughts. I drop my pen when I realize it's my phone and I have no idea where it is buried. I shuffle some papers and when I find it, I see that it's Ty.

"Tell me you have good news," I say immediately.

"The apartment is all mine. I got a great deal because they had just moved the mother out and wanted to be done so they could put the money aside for her nursing home care." I jump up from my chair and pump my fist in excitement. "Now, here's the part that you might not like as much." My excitement quickly fades, and I sit back into my chair and throw my head back.

"Let me hear it," I say with a sigh.

"While I'm finishing up here, I was hoping you

could take the lead on getting my place set up so I can hit the ground running when I get there."

I hang my head in defeat because I know he knows I won't say no to him. Little Assistant to the rescue like always. I don't know how many things he's roped me into over the years. I just went along with his schemes and crazy ideas. He knows he can always count on me because I've never told my big brother no.

"You know I'll do it."

"I knew I could count on you. The moving company is coming to get the equipment tomorrow so it should be there next Saturday."

"Email me all the details. And we're still not telling Mom?"

"I want to wait until I get there so I can see her face when we tell her."

"Got it. Did you know she's adding a shower to the basement bathroom?" I ask.

"She only talks to me about food plans and daughters-in-law," Ty responds.

"I get home improvements, physical ailments, and daughters-in-law." I laugh.

"Maybe we can work on finding some women when I get there. We were always good at finding women when we went out together. I don't seem to have the same luck without you."

"I might just have to be your wingman."

"I thought you bowed out with that girl."

"I *may* have taken your advice," I draw out.

"Is that so?" I can hear the smug look on his face.

"I went back to tell her that I wasn't giving up and that she could date both of us until she figured out I was the best option."

"That's my little bro!"

"Watch it." I warn.

"Seriously though, what did she say?"

"That the other guy wouldn't be a problem."

"Why not?" Ty asks.

I start cracking up at the memory and try to explain it to Ty. "The other guy was running out the door with his pants half zipped, no shirt, no shoes. I had a strong indication at that point that I had made the right choice to go back to talk to her."

"You think he naked-manned her?" Ty is laughing now.

"That would be my guess. She was all flustered when I got there. As she let me in, I noticed she had spilled some red wine and I, being a crime writer, hammed it up and pretended it was blood. Told her she should have rolled him up in the carpet so we could get rid of the body and the blood."

"Dude, you didn't. That poor girl. I would have kicked you out immediately."

"I think she might have wanted to at first but then I

told her I was joking and we had a good laugh. I love that she gets my humor. I helped her clean it up, asked her out to dinner, and left after she agreed," I finish abruptly.

"Hold up. I know that tone…what aren't you telling me?"

"That was pretty much it."

"No, it's not. Spill," Ty demands. I huff out a sigh.

"We may have almost kissed. I had her in my arms, but she backed away and said she had to finish cleaning up, so I let her go."

"Dude."

"I had a hard time walking home."

"No doubt," he says.

"But I'm taking her to a nice dinner Tuesday night, so I'm hoping I'll get a kiss then."

"Since you're so *suave,* you're going to have to help me next."

"Follow the Hudson way and I'll lead you to love," I jest.

"Oh, wise, Love Guru, I will follow you and your wisdom. Thank you for taking on a lowly meathead," Ty jokes in a melodramatic tone then quickly changes the subject. "Have you looked her up?"

"Why would I?"

"Bro, you were worried about a stage five clinger and now you're casually joking about blood? What happened to you?”

"I don't know, Ty. There's just something about her. I can't get her out of my mind. I just want to be near her all the time. It's like I thrive off her energy. When I got back from the park the other day, I was jotting down notes and my mind was racing with new ideas like I had been shocked and it unleashed all my creativity at one time. I could barely write fast enough." I'm envisioning her face right now when Ty cuts in with his usual ribbing.

"It's called a keyboard. It's this new invention. Makes writing faster." Ty deadpans.

"Ha. Ha. You know the first notes are always hand-written. It is the way." Ty laughs at my *Mandalorian* reference.

"All right, I've got to go get everything labeled for the movers, so keep me posted and I'll send you the info."

"Sounds good," I say, disregarding all the work I have to do and thinking about how Tuesday can't come fast enough.

CHAPTER FOURTEEN
Allison

AFTER AN EVENTFUL weekend that included an almost kiss, I head to the post office to see what goodies I have for today. While I walk in the brisk autumn weather, I think about Daveed and how he could ever think that me inviting him up for wine equaled pulling a naked-man on me. Then Oliver telling me I could date them both. Then him teasing me about the wine spill. He totally had me going at first, but seeing how funny he was gave him major brownie points. I'm still laughing to myself when I walk into the post office and am assaulted with the weird paper smell that only a post office can provide. Stuffed in my P.O. Box is a thick, brown envelope from a client and a notice to pick up a box. When the postal worker hands me the box, I see that it's from Granite Fitness and know that it's the protein powder samples I've been waiting for to finish Grant's site.

When I return to my apartment, I set the box on the

kitchen table and open the brown envelope. It's the first few chapters of the book my client is working on. She said she'd send me what she had so far because she was excited with how her website turned out. I set the chapters on my bedside table where I already have a stack of books waiting to be read. I always have good intentions to read before bed, but nothing pulls me as much as an Oliver Hudson book. "I promise I'll read you all," I say to the books and then return to the kitchen to open the box from Grant. The packets are black with the name ProAmp in all-caps, bold gold lettering at the top, and "Muscle Building Protein Shake," in white below. The directions on the back of the packet say one scoop of powder with a cup of milk or water. There are two servings per sample pack.

I can't wait to try the shakes. Grant was so excited about them, and if I could actually have a plan for lunch that doesn't involve running to the market every afternoon, I'm all for it. I set the packet down on the kitchen counter and drag out my full-size blender from my corner cabinet while considering why I don't have a BlendJet. I didn't write the product description for those, but I'm a believer, and pretty sure I need one in all the colors because I can't decide which one I like the best.

I try the chocolate first because you can never go wrong with chocolate. I've been burned by vanilla before and am always hesitant when trying a new version. As

I'm mixing, the phone rings from where I accidentally left it in my office. I quickly grab a reusable straw from the drain basket and plop it into the large, non-portable blender pitcher, carrying it with me as I run to my desk.

"Moore Than Words, how may I help you? Yes. Certainly. I'll send over my information packet. Can I have your email?" As I'm jotting down the address, I take a sip of the shake. *Blech.* I spew the shake all over my desk. I'm mortified because my potential new client just heard that. "I'm so sorry. Pardon me."

"Are you all right?" the customer asks.

I'm grabbing tissues and trying to wipe my tongue clean of the evilness I just ingested and trying to remain as professional as possible.

"Yes, sorry, I just had a slight issue with my drink. What was your email address again?" I grab one of the few pens and a Post-it pad that escaped the liquid assault and write down the email. "Thank you. I'll send it right over."

I quickly hang up and dry heave on my way to the kitchen to get some water to remove the awful taste from my mouth. I go straight to the sink and use the hose to power wash the film off my tongue. There is no time for the formalities of drinking from a cup. I cannot let the evil get absorbed into my body. What in the ever-loving hell is in that? I grab the package and read the ingredients. Nothing jumps out at me as being strange, but the protein count is high so maybe that aftertaste is meat. That's it! It tastes like chocolate-flavored meat! I have no idea how I'm going to write about this. *You're a professional so you will pretend it's the most creamy delicious shake you've ever tasted.* I grab some towels to clean off my desk. Once that's all taken care of, I retrieve a cookie from my stash of goodies in the pantry and some soda to get this taste out of my mouth and my memory before I can do any work. Once my body is happy again, I can focus. I send the email packet off as promised, then get started on the protein shake.

High-quality whey protein…that tastes like a blended chocolate cow.

Probably shouldn't go with that. After starting and deleting and retyping several times I think I finally have the description the way I want it. I finish up the rest of the items on my list for Granite Fitness and read over it once more before sending it off to Grant. He's going to see the email and call me to hear what I think about the shake and I have no idea what I'm going to say. I don't want to lie to him, but I can't hurt his feelings either. I don't want to burst his happy bubble. I'll just tell him the same thing I wrote in the description: it was creamy and delicious. Or maybe I can just not answer the phone and tell him I'm extremely busy.

The phone rings exactly thirty-two seconds after sending the email.

"Hi, Grant," I greet.

"What? I'm not handsome today?"

"I can't see you, so I don't know."

"You haven't seen me any other day. Why the formality?"

"Oh, I was looking over an email when the phone rang. I wasn't thinking."

"Uh, huh. I see you got the shake and finished the write-up. Thank you. I'm so glad you liked it."

"I *surely* did," I enthusiastically cheer.

"You didn't like it did you?"

"Why would you ask that?"

"Do you remember when you broke up with Roger and word vomited on me? And remember when you got that big client and were so nervous but knocked it out of the park?" he asks.

"I seem to recall those events. What's your point?" I fiddle with the pen on my desk.

"I was there for all of that, and I know your voice. You don't have to lie to me."

"Fine," I huff, throwing my hands in the air then bringing them over my eyes. "I'm sorry Grant. I didn't care for it. It tasted like chocolate meat," I squeak out. He starts laughing at my description and I'm so happy I haven't completely hurt his feelings.

"That's a new one," he admits between laughs.

"I didn't offend you?" I ask, removing my hands from my face and looking out the window as we talk.

"No. There are tons of shakes out there because everyone is different and have different tastes. The one you tried is for bodybuilders, so it's packed with protein. The next round will be more for the everyday person who just needs a healthy meal option on the go. You may like that better. Actually, I should have you come do some taste tests with me."

"Really? Wow, that would be fun, and we'd finally get to meet face-to-face!"

"Yeah, the test kitchen is here in California, but I'm going to be in New York soon. I'm hoping I could take you out to dinner when I come."

Holy flooping shirtballs.

"I'd like that very much. When will you be coming?"

"In a couple weeks," he says.

"Oh wow. Well, let me know when it gets closer. I'm not going anywhere so I should be around."

"Great. I'll talk to you soon. Bye, Allison."

"Bye, handsome," I respond.

"There's my girl," I hear Grant whisper before I hang up the phone. *My girl?* Oh my gosh, have I gone too far with my flirting? I never thought Grant would ever come here. That we'd ever meet. I have a date with Oliver. I genuinely like him and after the Daveed debacle I don't want Oliver thinking I'm some sort of player. I need to stop overthinking. He was just flirting like he normally does. That's all.

CHAPTER FIFTEEN

Oliver

I STOP AT a flower shop before my date with Ally. Amongst the display of elaborate sprays and pick-your-own items, a bouquet of pink and red peonies catches my eye. The man behind the counter wraps them up in brown paper and twine for me, and I head to Ally's apartment.

"Hi." Her smile lights up the dim hallway when she opens the door to her apartment. She is breathtaking. Her long auburn hair is straight and shiny, her hazel eyes sparkle, and her green dress hugs all her curves to perfection.

"Hi," I echo while stepping into her apartment as she steps back to let me in. "These are for you." I hand her the peonies.

"They're beautiful. I love the colors, and they're one of my favorite flowers," she says while giving me a welcoming hug. "You're also right on time. I love that."

"Of course. I hate to be late. I find it disrespectful of

the other person's time."

"Two points for Oliver," she cheers.

"Are you keeping some kind of score?"

"I'm going to be straight up honest with you. I'm not very trusting. It takes me a while to let down my guard and while you have been a perfect gentleman when we're together, I'd just like to make sure you are, in fact, not a psycho killer."

"I thought you'd figured out by now that I'm not."

"Or I'd be dead already?" she laughs.

"I'm glad you have a sense of humor. I really did have to do research for my books, you probably never want to see my search history, but it's all fiction. My mother would have my head if I weren't a perfect gentleman to any woman."

"I think I like your mother. So where are we going tonight?"

"Martino's," he says. "Have you been?"

"No. I've heard good things though."

"Their food is amazing. You'll love it. It's a special place to me. Are you ready to go?"

"Yes." I help her into it her jacket, then she grabs her purse before locking up.

WHEN THE CAB pulls up in front of Martino's, the warm

glow of the Edison bulbs give off a welcoming, homey feeling, and I can't wait to share this experience with her.

I take her hand to help her out of the cab and don't let go. She doesn't pull away and we walk hand in hand into the restaurant and to the table. We pass several white linen-covered tables with fine china plates and crystal candle holders in the middle of each one. The dim lighting continues the cozy feel of the lights outside and gives off a romantic vibe.

"This place is beautiful," she says as I pull out her chair for her and she takes a seat on the curved back, leather chair.

"Yes. It makes me feel like I'm back in Italy," I tell her as I take mine.

"You've been?" she asks.

"Yes. Have you?"

"I've never been out of the country," she admits.

"We need to remedy that."

"How so?" She lifts an eyebrow. "Are you going to take me?"

"Maybe. But you'd have to be my girlfriend first, so I guess it depends on how this date goes," I jest.

"Girlfriend, huh? You think dangling a trip to Italy will make me instantly sign up for that role?" She sits up straight and places her hand on her hip.

I hold out my hand. "That's not what I meant at all. It's just that Italy is so romantic that I'd like to experience it with a special someone the next time I go. I wasn't putting any pressure on you at all."

"Oh." She places her napkin on her lap and looks at the menu. I feel like her response wasn't her normal playful banter.

"Ally, did I say something wrong?" She looks over the top of the menu at me.

She holds up her hand in apology. "I'm sorry. My last serious boyfriend was controlling and I started to lose myself but thankfully we broke up before it went too far. So, I'd just like to see how things go naturally and not use labels so quickly."

"I see. I'd like to take things at whatever speed you are comfortable with. No pressure." I sit back in my chair and adjust the napkin on my lap.

"So, if I said I wanted to take you on this table right now, you'd be okay with it?" she jokes.

"I'd be happy to honor the lady's wishes. However, I would prefer a more secluded area." We both laugh. "In all sincerity though, I'm not like that at all. I want you to know that when I hold the door open for you or pull out your chair it's a sign of respect. I know you are a modern woman capable of doing such things on your own, but I want you to know you are special to me and that's why I do it."

"Thank you," she says, and I leave it at that, knowing I got my point across. She looks back down at the menu.

"Do you know what you'd like to have?"

"How about you pick," she says.

"Did you not just say you don't like controlling men?"

"Yes, but you've been here before, and I'd like to have your favorite dish." She hands me her menu looking pleased with herself and sits back.

"You got it!" When the waiter comes, I order fried zucchini with their garlic aioli sauce, Fettuccini Alfredo with meatballs, and a large Caesar salad.

"I've never had fettuccine with meatballs before."

"You'll be glad I ordered. Their sauces are homemade delicious goodness, and I could eat the meatballs all by themselves, but the marinara sauce they are cooked in mixes with the Alfredo and creates this rose sauce and—" Allison reaches out and wipes my chin with her napkin.

"You had a little drool coming out there." She laughs, letting me know she's just teasing me.

"I wouldn't be surprised if there was. It's my favorite meal. And wait till you try the fresh rolls they bring."

"Can't wait."

"Did you want any wine?" I ask.

"I would, but since the last time I had wine didn't go over so well, I'll stick with the water. Thank you for making a bad situation better."

"My pleasure. So, besides yoga, what else are you interested in?"

"I also do Tai Chi and eat small individual meals because I hate leftovers."

"As someone who benefits from you foregoing leftovers, I approve of this interesting preference."

"Is it so fascinating?" She raises a brow.

"I think so. I think those little things are what make people interesting. It's where their personalities and character evolve from. Maybe it's just the writer in me."

"I know what you mean, the little things can add up to a lot of big things."

"Tell me more about your job and these samples you get," I say with a wink, remembering how I had to carry a box of sex toys down two, egregiously long city blocks.

"Are you referring to any samples in particular?" She blushes.

"Perhaps." I grin, egging her on.

"They aren't all as fun as that box."

"Fun? So, you tried them?" I ask.

"I…Well…Uh…You know." I give her the, you've been caught, look. "Fine!" she huffs. "Yes. I did. But only one…and only once," she rushes out.

"And?"

"And what?" she asks as if she doesn't know what I'm getting at.

"And, did they get a good review from you?" Her cheeks turn bright red, and she stares at her lap.

"If you must know, all my products get good write-ups because that's my job. It's not a review, it's a description about the product, so it's always positive and informative," she clarifies, straightening her back and looking me in the eye.

"Gotcha." I muffle a laugh behind my napkin.

"For example," she continues and I look at her with a serious face. "I just worked on a protein shake that was absolutely disgusting."

"What's it called? You know, so I can steer clear of it."

"Liquid Moo," she announces with a straight face, but then her eyes get big and she suddenly can't control her laughter. The sound is a jolt to my system. I start laughing along with her. We get some stares from the other tables, but I couldn't care less because I'm having a great time with Ally. Once she's composed herself again, she gives me a serious look.

"Actually, I'd rather not say. He's a personal trainer I work with. Great guy. He's starting his own line of products for his clients. He works in California. I just updated his website, and he said since I didn't care for this shake, I could help him taste test the next round of them. I'm actually excited about it. I'll get to fly out there. Maybe I'll tell you once I approve of his recipe."

"Fly out to California to meet up with some guy who's all fit?" I ask, testing the waters.

"Oh, it would be strictly professional of course." She

sits up and pats my arm for reassurance.

"Uh, huh. Do you know anything about this guy? I mean, you were worried I was a psycho killer, so how do you know he's not?"

"Not too much. He dates models, so clearly, I wouldn't be his cup of tea."

"Why would you say that? You're gorgeous." She rolls her eyes.

"That's kind of you to say, but we all have things we don't like about ourselves."

"I'm sure models feel the same way. Everything on display, trying to look perfect all the time," I explain, trying to make her feel better.

"True. I might not love my imperfections but I'm glad I can enjoy dessert every once in a while."

I'm looking at her and I don't see any imperfections. But I can see where the last guy did a number on her because someone as kind, funny, and beautiful as she is should not have any confidence issues.

"Anyway," she continues, "he seems sweet, and we chat about his business, and sometimes his personal life, but I tend to talk more than he does. If you can imagine." She laughs at her self-deprecation. "Plus, didn't you watch *Legally Blonde*? Endorphins make you happy and happy people don't kill people." She gives me a wicked grin, and I know she's back to playful Ally and have nothing to worry about.

"That is true, but no I haven't," I admit sheepishly.

"You haven't watched *Legally Blonde*? And you write crime fiction? It's about a lawyer!"

"It looked a little too girly for me."

"Oh, macho man, we are soooo watching it together!"

"Bossy, bossy," I tease her.

"I mean, you don't have to if you don't want to," she fake pouts. "It would involve popcorn, a couch, and some snuggling in the dark, but hey, if you don't want to, that's okay. I wouldn't want you to do anything you didn't want to do." She gives me a sly smile and sits back in her chair. *Did she just let her guard down?*

I don't have a chance to respond because the appetizer arrives and we dig in.

CHAPTER SIXTEEN
Allison

THE FRIED ZUCCHINI is crispy and delicious. I don't know what they put in this garlic sauce but I'm ready to take some home and lick it off Oliver.

As I've watched him talk, all the other diners have faded away and I am hanging on his every word. He has a casual ease about himself. I enjoy being with him and we've had great conversations that flow as if they were mini stories. His mouth also comes to a natural smile when he isn't talking, and it makes you want to admit all your faults knowing that he'll still love you in spite of them all. *Almost.*

"So, Oliver," I start, twirling my first bite of fettuccine around my fork.

"Yes?" His brows perk up in anticipation of my question.

"This is truly the best fettuccine you've ever had? Like this is about to knock my socks off?"

"Are you wearing socks?" He quickly looks down at

my feet.

I laugh. "It's a figure of speech. I'm sure you've heard of that before, being a writer and all?" I wink.

"Oh, yes, yes, I think I have. And to answer your question, you're lucky you aren't wearing any socks because they would definitely be knocked off."

"Okay, here goes." I take a bite of the twirled pasta and my taste buds explode. "Oh my gosh, that's practically orgasmic," I admit covering my mouth while talking around a mouthful of noodles.

"I don't think I've ever heard food described that way. I may have to use that in my next book."

"This is seriously the best thing I've had in my whole life. I may never eat anywhere else again," I say, pointing to my plate with my fork.

"I'm glad you like it." He grins.

"I'll try not to moan too loud over here." I cover my mouth with my hand.

"Now I know the way to your heart," he says as I remove my hand.

"Yep. I'm not ashamed to admit this one. You can come over any time if you bring this with you."

He whips out an imaginary notepad and writes a note.

"Noted." He makes a gesture like he just dotted an *I*.

"What else should I know? Tell me a random fact about yourself." I take a few more bites of the pasta while he thinks.

"I have one I think you'd like."

"Tell me." I put my fork down and rest my head on my hand while staring him directly in the eyes waiting with bated breath.

"I'm a trained masseuse."

"No way." I tap the table in disbelief. "You're going to have to give me the background on that one." I lean back and continue eating.

"I had decided that my victim would be killed during their massage so I wanted to get a feel for how it would be in the room. I joined a class and then shadowed at a spa for a while."

"I can't believe you did all that in the name of research. Did you ever give anyone a massage?" I ask, captivated.

"I had a few people, who regularly volunteer at the massage school, agree to let me work on them."

My mouth falls open and I'm glad I didn't have a mouth full of fettuccini at the moment.

"Some of the people were disappointed I wasn't going to actually get certified," he continues.

I wipe my mouth and lean in. "I'd be very interested in feeling those fingers on me some time," I flirt.

He wiggles his fingers.

"Oh, you would, huh? That's very good to know." He winks.

I'm truly having the best time with him. He's funny, sarcastic, and flirty. I'm secretly thanking Daveed for showing, *ha showing*, me his true colors so I could focus solely on Oliver.

"Now it's your turn. What's your random fact?"

"You remember how I said I do Tai Chi? Well, I'm actually a second-degree black belt in taijutsu."

"You're kidding."

"Nope. I use Tai Chi to sound less scary to people." I shake my head and smile as he lets the fact sink in.

"Wow, I guess I don't have to worry about you when I'm not around."

"Now that we've gotten to know each other a little better, I will admit that while you don't *have* to worry about me, it's nice to know you want to. It's always nice to know someone will be wanting to know you got home okay. Usually that someone is Morgan for me."

"When you become my official girlfriend, I won't even have to think about it, I will always naturally worry about you."

"When?"

"I think you and I both know it's *when* not *if.*"

I sit back in my chair as the waiter clears our plates and smile at Oliver. I like his confidence. Once we're alone again I sit forward, reach for his hand, and intertwine our fingers.

"I do." I smile and he smiles in return as we stare

into each other's eyes. The trance is broken when we're offered dessert menus.

"I'm too stuffed. Can we take a raincheck on dessert?" I ask.

"Sure. Just the check please," he says to the waiter and then looks back at me.

"Thank you for a fabulous meal."

"You're welcome. You sure you don't want the leftovers?" I glare at him, and he laughs.

"You mentioned that we *would*, in fact, be dating. I'm going to assume this was date number one, so how about I cook dinner for you and we watch *Legally Blonde* as date number two?" I ask.

"I would say that sounds like a good idea. Even if I don't like the movie, I'll be with you, so it won't be all bad."

"Oh, it's not an *if* you will like it, you *will*. It's hilarious. You just have to not take it seriously."

"Gotcha. Can't wait. When should I come over?" he asks.

"How about Friday?"

"It's a plan."

Oliver pays the bill and we hail a cab back to my place where he walks me to my door. I pause and jingle my keys, wondering if the trick I learned while watching *Hitch*, actually works. When I look up, Oliver is standing close and looking down at me. And…I'm pretty sure he's coming in his ninety percent.

"May I?" he whispers.

I don't answer. I just lean the last ten percent and place my lips on his. He cradles my face in his hands as he gently kisses me. When his tongue teases my lips, I part them and sigh, letting him in. Our kiss goes from sweet to intense in point five seconds. I run my hands through his hair at the nape of his neck while he moves his hands to hold the back of my head. My head spins and my nerves buzz with electricity. Just as I'm about to invite him in, he breaks our kiss, gives me a hug, and bids me goodnight.

I watch him walk down the stairs before I float into my apartment on a love cloud.

CHAPTER SEVENTEEN

Oliver

WHEN I ARRIVE at Ally's door with a new bundle of peonies in hand, the aroma of roasted meat and fresh bread seeps out from under the door. My mouth waters as I rap on the wood. There is a pattering of socked feet before the door opens. Ally is standing in an oversized college sweatshirt over black leggings and slouchy socks on her feet. Her hair is in a high ponytail and there's a twinkle in her eyes. She looks adorable.

"You look terrific," I tell her.

She eyes me then the flowers I'm holding.

"I can't cook in nice clothes. I have to be comfortable. Are those for me?"

"Nope." Her face falls for half a second before I start to laugh. "Of course they are. I figured the other ones were getting old by now."

"They're beautiful. Come on in. Dinner is almost ready. I made a roast and popped some rolls in the oven. My mom told me it would be the easiest thing to make and I just threw everything in a pot."

"It smells delicious."

"Could you swap out the flowers in the vase in my bedroom while I get the table ready?"

"Sure thing."

I find the vase on the side table by her bed and notice a stack of books next to it. My latest release is sitting on top, so I quickly grab the pen next to the stack and sign it for her. Then I take the vase back into the kitchen to change out the bouquet and put the new one back in her room.

When I walk back into the kitchen she says, "Thank you. I love seeing them when I wake up in the morning."

"I'm glad they bring you joy."

"They certainly do." She wipes the counter and turns to me. "Everything is ready."

"Great. Let me wash my hands first. The bathroom is on the left, right?"

"Second door. Uh, Olly?" I turn back to look at her.

"Yes?"

"You are just going to wash your hands, right?" she asks nervously.

We both share a look and then burst out laughing.

"I will come back fully clothed until you tell me otherwise." I hold up my hand in Scout's honor formation.

"What can I get you to drink while you're in there?"

"Wine. Water. Whatever," I respond.

"Whatever coming right up," she sasses.

When I get back to the table, the meat is sliced on a platter with potatoes and carrots encircling the edges. Warm rolls are in a basket covered with a cloth napkin, and there is red wine and a glass of water next to each plate.

"This looks wonderful. I appreciate you cooking for me."

"Of course. Just don't get used to it." She gives me a raised brow before she places food on my plate. "I can cook spaghetti, but we just had it, so I had to come up with another plan."

"I don't cook much either. Thank goodness for Joe's and the market."

"Same here. It's no fun to cook for just one person." She takes a big sip of wine and sets down her glass.

"So..." she starts.

"Yes?" I raise my brow.

"In a rom-com, this would probably be the time they'd unload their past baggage. Do you want to tell me about your last serious relationship and why it didn't work out?"

"Wow. You get right to the point. Why not?" I set my fork down and wipe my mouth. "My ex is actually my ex-fiancée. She was beautiful on the outside but not always on the inside. She had her, what I call, monster moments, but I felt like I could balance her out because she always said I made her be a better person."

"Can I ask what happened?"

"I had proposed. She said yes. But about a week before the wedding she called it off. Her parents were furious, but she said she could never live up to my expectations and she knew she couldn't commit to me for the rest of her life."

"Wow." She makes an "o" with her lips as she says it.

"What were your expectations? Should I be concerned?" She squints and I can't tell if she's being sarcastic or not.

"To love me and be a nice person?" I shrug.

"Whoa, whoa, whoa, you need to curb those expectations at the door, mister." I see the laughter starting in her eyes and laugh with her. "That doesn't sound like a bad deal," she says after we compose ourselves.

"We all have our baggage that the right person will overlook and love us in spite of. I thought I gave her that, but she couldn't give it back to me." Ally rubs my arm.

"I'm sure that sucked in the moment but look where you are now. I think you made out for the better." She leans back and points to herself.

"I couldn't agree more. This roast is delicious," I say, forking another piece into my mouth.

"Have as much as you want. You know you'll be

taking the leftovers home."

"But if I have leftovers, I won't have to go to the market, and I might miss a chance to see you."

"Then you'll just have to come here again instead."

"Anytime you want me, I'll be here."

"I'm going to hold you to it," she quips.

"I believe it's your turn to tell me about your ex now."

"Just because you shared doesn't mean I have to."

"True. But I'd love to know what I should avoid doing in the future." I take out my imaginary pen and notepad and give her my full attention.

"Just let me be me. With Roger, I always had to be perfect. I had to do things on his schedule. If he was late, I had to be ready and waiting. If I was late, he'd be furious, saying I didn't value his time.

"And those dinner parties for his work people were the worst. I had to be dressed just so. He'd always pick out the outfit and leave it for me to put on before he went to work. I was basically his arm candy, and no one really talked to me or asked me much. Even the other wives and girlfriends kept quiet. It was a Stepford wives type of vibe when we were there. I'd ask him about it, and he'd brush it off.

"One time I spoke up and asked one of the gentlemen a question, and you would have thought I'd slapped him in the face instead. Roger quickly excused us and whisked me out of there so fast, I barely stayed on my feet. That's when I knew there was something seriously wrong with him, his job, and his expectations, so I broke it off with him.

"He didn't even argue. Said he agreed that I wasn't up to his standards and if I hadn't said something first, he would have.

"That was it and I'm thankful every day that it wasn't something worse or physical."

"Now it's my turn to say it…wow." I emphasize the word because I can't believe there are guys still out there like that.

"Yep. Now you can see why I keep my guard up. It's hard to be trusting. He was perfect on paper. Handsome. Successful. Had his own car. His own apartment. Showed interest in what I said…at first. I guess at the time we met he was trying to gauge if I fit his narrative."

"I hope I can show you I'm not like that. I'm enjoying our time together." It's my turn to rub her arm.

"Me too. And you already are." She squeezes my arm in reassurance.

I look at her hand and then up into her eyes. She smiles, and that's when I feel it. That's when I know she's let me in. And I know I never want to make her frown. My eyes linger, and I lean in to give her a kiss. A soft kiss. A kiss that lets her know I'll never hurt her. When we break away, I look down at the table.

"Let me help you clean this up and we can get the movie started."

"We can just throw everything in the dishwasher and get our snuggle on," she says, wiggling her hips.

"Love it."

Once we're all set on the couch she snuggles into my shoulder, and I couldn't care less what's on the screen.

CHAPTER EIGHTEEN

Allison

I'M LYING IN bed staring at the peonies next to me, daydreaming about last night, and kinda, maybe wishing Oliver had spent the night. Before he got there, I had set up a goodie box of sweet treats on the coffee table and had assorted sodas chilling in the fridge to have while watching the movie after dinner. We had both picked grape soda, so I made one big cup and added two straws for sharing. I microwaved some popcorn, and we enjoyed all the snacks while we watched *Legally Blonde,* and he gave commentary on how none of this would actually happen. I had to remind him it's a rom-com and it's supposed to be silly. I may have started a tickle fight that ended up with me pinned under his hard body—I did not imagine him being so fit—invoking a frantic make-out session. I almost asked him to stay.

I can't seem to pry myself out of bed today wishing I was curled up next to Oliver instead of my body pillow. It surprises me that I opened up so quickly with him, but he's refreshingly different. He's not demanding. He genuinely cares about what I have to say. He makes everything easy. He even watched *Legally Blonde* for me. And I could tell he secretly enjoyed it. I sigh and roll onto my back knowing not much is getting done today. I eventually get out of bed and stretch my arms over my head before walking to the kitchen for breakfast. As I'm pouring my coffee there is a sudden commotion in the hallway.

"Hold up! You're going to hit the wall with the end of that. Pivot! Step up! Now straight back," I hear hollered outside my apartment door. Sounds like the new tenant is moving in. I peek out the peephole of my door and all I see is the back of a man's head. As he moves away, I see him carry something very large and very heavy, based on the way he and the other man are lumbering, into the doorway across the hall. There are moving blankets draped over the item, so I can't see what it is, probably just a dresser or entertainment cabinet. I'm super curious and I run to my closet to throw on some running gear that I got to sample when I worked on an athleisure site. My apartment overlooks the alley in the back of the building, so I can't see the moving van. I think I'll go stretch a bit out front to see what I can find out.

I peek through the open door of the apartment across the hall to see if the new tenant might be inside as I pull my door shut. No luck. I'm about to turn for the steps and am almost run over by a mover carrying several boxes.

"Pardon me, little lady," he quips as he passes.

"No problem, sir. Have a good day," I call over my shoulder as I bound down the stairs to the front stoop, narrowly avoiding being run over by the next load. I move to the side and bend at my waist to start stretching the backs of my legs.

As I'm snooping upside down through my legs, I notice most items have been unloaded and look around for the owner, but only see the men in gray overalls stacking boxes to take upstairs.

"Well now, that's a view I don't mind seeing first thing in the morning." Oliver's voice jolts me to a standing position, and I whirl around to face him.

"Oliver! What are you doing here?"

"I'm moving in, baby!"

"What?" I know I wanted him to stay over last night, but do I want him living across the hall from me? I can feel my face contorting with different emotions.

"I'm just kidding, don't freak out." He holds out his hands. "I'm not moving in, my brother is. When I left your apartment a few weeks ago, I ran into the realtor and asked to see the place. It's a perfect setup for him."

"Why didn't you tell me?"

"I didn't want to say anything until it was all done. I

was coming to see you but then got sidetracked when I saw a very cute butt up in the air. You know you really shouldn't go waving that around in just anyone's direction." He laughs.

"I was trying to be sneaky, make it look like I was stretching."

"Oh, I see. A yoga detective, now that's an interesting idea."

"You write true crime, not cozy mysteries. I'm not sure that will work."

"Oh, there are all kinds of characters you can write in to move the story along, she could be a witness." He winks. "It's getting chilly out here, do you want to grab some coffee? We're all done here for the moment. I'll start setting things up when we get back."

"Okay, that sounds great. You can tell me more about your brother. Who did you say was cuter?" I jest.

"I am, now let's go." Oliver gives me a quick peck on the lips, and we walk to Joe's hand-in-hand.

CHAPTER NINETEEN
Oliver

AS WE WALK to get coffee, I realize I'm completely and utterly falling in love with this bold, funny, incredible woman. I hold the door open, and the waft of freshly brewed coffee and baked goods invade my senses. I let her walk in first and she holds her hands up to form a heart at the barista.

"What was that?" I laugh.

"Oh, Katelyn and I have hand codes when she sees me walk in. I always hold up two fingers when Morgan joins me, so now that there are still two of us, but you aren't Morgan, I make a heart, so she knows it's my boyfriend and not Morgan with me."

"Boyfriend?"

"What can I get you?" Katelyn asks me before I can get an answer from Ally.

"Medium mocha latte, please." I turn back to Ally.

"Yeah, why not?" She shrugs. "I think you can say after last night we've gotten to a new level in our relationship."

I can't hide the joy I feel and agree. "I will admit that I will never think of that movie in the same way ever again. I couldn't be happier that you want me to be your boyfriend, but I thought you didn't want to rush into labeling anything."

"I didn't, but now I do." She bops my nose with her finger and walks to the other end of the counter.

"I'm glad you do." I give her a quick kiss, a smile undeniably forming on my face.

We grab our coffees from the pickup counter and walk to Ally's table at the front of the cafe to sit.

"Now that we have our relationship status settled. Tell me more about your brother." She holds onto my free hand while taking a sip of her coffee.

"When I moved to the city to write, Ty moved to California to start his personal training business. Now he wants to open a place here for when his celebrity clients travel back and forth between the coasts. I'm so excited he's coming back. I can't wait to introduce you two. You're going to love him."

Ally releases my hand and starts to fidget with the cup sleeve on her coffee, "What's his name again?"

"Ty."

I notice her shoulders relax and she sits back in her chair. "So, when does he get here?" She nervously fiddles with her hair.

"In about a week or so. He doesn't have a set date since I'm helping him. He's going to work out of his apartment and then will look for a retail space when he gets here. I was lucky to have run into that realtor so I didn't have to traipse all over the city looking for a place. And it's going to be convenient having you guys in one building."

"Yes, that will be fun." Her words are light, but her body language is off.

"Everything okay? You suddenly seem tense."

"Yep, I'm perfect." She raises her cup as if to toast. I decide to let it drop for now and give her free hand a reassuring squeeze.

"Enough about Ty. Let's talk about you and me. I was thinking about coming over tonight and giving you a massage." Her demeanor suddenly changes and a big smile spreads across her face.

"Oh, I'd like that very much, boyfriend." She wiggles in her seat.

"How about I order us some dinner and then get you naked, girlfriend?"

"I think I could get behind that plan."

"It's a date. Let's get back. I've got to start setting up the apartment."

"And I'll get everything prepped for tonight." She winks.

I walk her back to her apartment and then go across

the hall to Ty's. Thankfully everything was well-labeled, and the big equipment is already placed where it needs to be to match Ty's mapped-out floor plan. I would have never been able to move it on my own. I clap my hands and rub them together as I decide where to start. I'll tackle the gym area since that's what he'll need done first. No one will need to go back into the bedrooms. However, knowing Ty, maybe I *should* do his room first. I laugh to myself and decide to stay with the original plan and start with the gym.

CHAPTER TWENTY
Allison

I WALK INTO my apartment and completely freak out. What are the odds that I work with a celebrity personal trainer and so is Oliver's brother? I know their names are different but I'm slightly freaking out. I decide to call Grant and see if he knows this Ty guy. He doesn't answer. I'm not exactly sure what I want to say anyway, so it's best to wait until I can speak to him in person or over the phone or maybe actually in person. My mind is spinning. I need Morgan.

"Hey Hooker, what's up?"

"I'm not a hooker, I'm a girlfriend. I don't sleep with more than one guy, why do you always call me that?"

"Whoa, we've always joked about that, what's going on?"

"Well, I'm having a slight crisis." I plop on my couch and draw my knees up to my chest.

"I'm sorry, please go on."

"Guess who's moving into Mrs. G's apartment?" I

say, slightly freaking out.

"No way. Oliver is going to live across the hall from you?" Morgan ventures.

"Worse, his brother." I hug my legs.

"How exactly is that worse, you don't even know him?"

"I might."

"What? How?"

"I think it might be Grant." I drop my feet to the floor and start pacing.

"Your phone crush? The one you thought you could never have because he lives in California?"

"Yes, that Grant."

"Is his name Grant?"

"No, it's Ty. But Morgan, he lives in California and trains celebrities. How many could there be?" I chew on my thumbnail.

"Lots! Do you think there is only one trainer in all of California for celebrities? I think you might just be stirring a pot of something that doesn't need to be stirred."

"You think?"

"Yes, clearly his brother isn't Grant. Grant hasn't said anything to you about moving here. There are tons of people in California, it's a big state. Even if he were from LA, the odds would have to be super low. His brother could be anyone. And besides, if it were him, why would it matter?"

"Oh, I don't know because I've had unprofessional banter with him and he knows stuff about me that Oliver doesn't know yet, and I've always crushed on him. And he might have mentioned he's coming to New York soon and wants to take me to dinner."

"Would you leave Oliver for him?"

"I don't think so."

"You don't think?"

"Oliver and I had an incredible date last night. I cooked—"

"You cooked? Why are we even having this conversation? You never cook. For anyone. This is serious."

"I know. I almost asked him to stay the night. I called him my boyfriend this morning!"

"So, why would you be worried about his brother moving in? It sounds like a non-issue to me."

"BECAUSE I've had a crush on this guy for years and you know how you always wonder if you're meant to be. What if I rushed things with Oliver? What if I'm actually meant to be with Grant!" I shake my arm in the air with each question.

"I seriously think you need to get your head on straight. Oliver is a great guy. Don't mess this up for some lofty dream. And I'm pretty sure this isn't the same guy. You need to chill."

"You're right. And he's coming to give me a massage

tonight."

"Explain to me again how this is at all fair? Daveed, Oliver, Grant."

I giggle. "It's not. Thank you for talking me off the ledge." I sit back down on the couch and take a deep breath.

"That's what I'm here for. Now you wanna throw one of the other two my way?"

"Morgan!"

"What? You said Daveed was packing. I would not have turned that down."

"You're terrible."

"You're worse. Go enjoy this amazing night your *boyfriend* has planned for you, and stop worrying about something that isn't even an issue. When's Grant coming anyway?"

"In a week or so depending on his schedule."

"You'll have to let me know when he gets here so I can call dibs. If he's half as cute as Oliver, I'm in."

"I definitely will. You know I've got your back. But now I've got to go get ready to get naked."

"Ugh, I hate you so much. Which bar did we find Daveed in?"

"I'm not telling because you need to find someone better. And, I love you too."

I hang up and feel better. I sound like a boy-crazy teenager. I have a great guy who wants to spoil me, so why am I having thoughts about another guy I haven't met before? I'm not. Not anymore. I'm one hundred percent committed to my new boyfriend, and now I must scrub, buff, and polish for this evening's events.

CHAPTER TWENTY-ONE
Allison

WHEN I GET out of the shower, I wrap myself in a robe and pad out to the kitchen for a glass of white wine. Just as I'm about to sit down on the couch to wait for Oliver, I hear banging and grunting outside my door.

I open it to find Oliver tossing boxes out of the door across the hall. I decide to lean on the door frame and watch his muscles flex with the exertion.

"Looks like I should be the one giving you a massage tonight." I startle him, and he pops up and turns to me.

"Oh, don't you worry about me. I want tonight to be all about you."

"Well, I can't argue with that. I do like having all the attention," I flirt.

"Hmm, come here." He pulls me toward him and presses his lips to mine.

They are tentative at first but when I wrap my arms around his neck and pull him closer, he brings the heat.

Hard, ravenous kisses turn into teasing kisses that let me know what his tongue is capable of, and I'm wishing that he was using it somewhere else. I moan and press my body against his. His hands curl into fists, gripping my robe at my waist, and I tug him toward my door.

"Oh no, you're going to have to wait," he says, pulling back. My lips are decidedly annoyed, and I pout.

"No fair, you're a tease."

"No way. You totally pressed against me. I just wanted a quick kiss before I got back to work."

"Uh huh, if you believe that you can fertilize the lawn." He laughs.

"Actually, hold on a sec." He leaves me, hot and bothered, standing in my doorway. I'm fanning myself with the collar of my robe when suddenly, he's shuffling out the door with a folded table in his hands.

"What's that?"

"It's a massage table. I forgot Ty had one. I can set it up and give you a proper massage."

"Oh."

"Why the long face?" he asks, registering my disappointment.

"I didn't think this was going to be quite the clinical massage the table suggests."

"Have I told you I like the way your mind works? And don't worry, sweetheart, I won't be professional tonight." He winks and proceeds into my apartment and sets up the table in the middle of my living room in front of the couch. Then he runs out and runs back in with a stack of pillows and sheets and finishes setting up the table. "Okay, we're all set. You drink your wine and I'll be back soon. I'm going to take a quick shower." He runs back out of my apartment and shuts the door behind him. Then I grab my glass and lounge on the couch in joyful bliss.

Fifteen minutes later, Oliver is back at my door in athletic shorts and a T-shirt. His dark hair tousled from the shower, and I just want to run my hands through it. So I do. I jump into his arms and run my fingers through it while we kiss.

"This is a new side of you I'm happy to see."

"Me too. This is the fun me. I really like you, Oliver. I'm glad you're my boyfriend."

"I'm glad you're my girlfriend. I like you too. Very much." He kisses me and then trails kisses down the side of my neck. I giggle because it tickles, and he puts me down. "What would you like for dinner?"

"You. I don't need to eat."

"Then get naked and get under those sheets while I warm up the oil and wash my hands." He rubs his hands together in anticipation and runs to the kitchen. "Oh, and face down first," he calls.

I drop my robe to the floor and climb onto the table face down, then pull the covers up to my shoulders.

"I'm ready," I sing out.

"I'm heating up the oil, just a few more minutes. Oh, hey do you have a Bluetooth speaker?"

"Yes, it's in my bedroom on my bookshelf."

"Okay, I'll grab it." I hear him go into my room, and then suddenly the apartment fills with the sound of spa music with different musical tones and sounds. I'm so glad he didn't pick the running water. That makes me have to pee. "Okay, sweetheart, I'm ready. Are you comfortable?"

"Very," I say and release a deep breath.

"Just relax and keep taking deep breaths."

I inhale and exhale while he gently runs his hands up and down my back. I immediately relax and let the music and his hands take me away.

He starts on my shoulders and works on the knots that have formed from typing on my laptop. There is a large knot on the right side and he bends his body closer to me to add pressure to the spot. His body heat ignites a spark, and it shoots down my spine. The soft music adds to the pleasure. It's as if he has choreographed his moves to the music. I want to speak and tell him how wonderful he is, but all I do is let out a contented sigh.

"That's it, let everything out. Breathe in the scented oils and breathe out the stress."

Oliver continues to massage my shoulders and back, moving the blankets down but his body heat keeps me warm. When he finishes my lower back, he covers me up and then moves the blankets to one side exposing my right buttock and leg. He gently kneads my butt and continues down to my leg.

"Your body is one continuous loop, so I have to massage everything for you to feel the full effect," he rumbles.

"Mmm hmm," I hum in a heady state of bliss.

As he's working on the pressure points in my feet a sharp pang hits my G-spot.

"Oh!" I jolt from the shock.

"I take it I found a good spot?" he teases, not waiting for an answer but continuing to rub the same place until something comes undone inside me and I writhe on the table. His magic hands keep me in place as they work up the back of my calves creating pure pleasure. I'm still tingling inside, and his firm hands working up and down my legs is an intoxicating sensation. Hard pressure as he works up to my butt, soft sweeps of his fingers as he works his way down. He does this several times, and each time he teases the ridge where my butt meets my thigh, and I want him to move those hands to my center. My core heats with need and I wiggle to let him know he can come in.

"Not yet," he whispers softly in my ear. "It's time to roll over Ally. I'll hold up the blanket for you while you reposition yourself."

I slowly roll onto my back, eager with anticipation of what's to come, and then he settles the blankets over my chest and tucks them under my arms. He then adjusts the bolster so that it's supporting the back of my knees to keep my back flat on the table.

He pauses to warm more oil between his hands before massaging my scalp. Tiny sparks dance across my head as his fingers move through my hair. In slow circular motions, he stimulates my scalp and works his way to my temples. The need he worked up in me is starting to subside as the music and his fingers lull me into a dream-like state. His hands have moved to my shoulders, rubbing and caressing.

"Deep breath in," he says, and I inhale at his command. "That's it. Now release." I exhale and fall further into a trance. "Deep breath in. Now release," he repeats.

After several rounds of deep breathing, I feel his hands move to my chest. Slowly circling…circling…circling until they are cupping my breasts. He is bent over me, his heat keeping me warm while he gently kneads my nipples in rhythm to the music, in rhythm to my breathing, in and out. The need returns and I let out a soft sigh as I slightly part my legs. He never stops touching me as he moves to the other end of the table near my feet. His hands cascading down my stomach like the decrescendo in the music. Over and over, lower and lower each time until he is at my entrance. I part my legs farther letting him know I'm ready. He teases my clit, and I quiver at his touch, but he continues to caress the sensitive skin until his rhythm makes me beg for him to enter me.

"Yeeesss," I breathe out.

His oiled finger slips into me. He strokes me in time with the drumbeat. Now two fingers. His thumb working my clit. Stroking…stroking. The drumbeat becomes louder and faster, the strokes become harder and faster in time until…until…I…I…am consumed in ecstasy. I whimper as his strokes slow and his fingers still inside me. Oliver lets out a deep breath and removes himself from me. He covers me up and runs his hands up and down my body over the blankets. I am relaxed and content once again.

Then he scoops me up off the table and carries me to my bed. I watch as he strips off his clothes and joins me under the covers. His magical hands are on me once more, and I run my hands over his back and down his sides, and then show him how magical mine can be. When he's ready, he allows me to take control, and I straddle over him and gently guide him in. Our bodies move in rhythm as we stare into each other's eyes. Connected to the core until euphoric sparks shoot through my body as I call out a boisterous yes. I continue to ride out the wave, and Oliver lets out a primal growl I've never heard before.

Once his body stills, I remove myself and lay by his side. Our matching breaths slowing until we fall asleep.

CHAPTER TWENTY-TWO

Oliver

I SLIP OUT from under the covers and throw away the tissue I wrapped the condom in before we fell asleep. The morning sun filters into her bathroom window, and I decide to run to Joe's for coffee and Danish for breakfast. Ally is still curled up in a ball like a kitten, wrapped in the covers and snuggled up next to my pillow as I get my clothes on.

I quickly shut and lock the door on my way out then jog down the steps. Katelyn sees me walk in and waves me over to the side to avoid the long line.

"Need anything else, O?" she asks, handing me our coffees.

"Could I get some cheese Danish?"

"Sure thing." She quickly grabs a bag and the Danish and whisks them back to me. After I pay, she's off to the next customer.

I let myself back in with Ally's key and set everything down on the kitchen counter.

"Oliver?" I hear Ally call.

"It's me, sweetheart. I ran and got us coffees," I reply, walking back into her bedroom.

"I thought I told you I don't need to eat," she says while removing her covers and showing me a heavenly sight.

I quickly strip off my clothes and pounce on top of her.

With a giggle from her, I reach for the condoms and begin round two.

We wake again around lunch time and my stomach is growling.

"Ally, I'm going to need some fuel to keep up with you. Are you okay with us getting some lunch delivered?"

"Yes, I'm hungry too. What did you say you got this morning?"

"Cheese Danish and coffee."

"Hmm, that sounds good. Let's have that while we wait for our lunch."

"You got it. What do you want for lunch?"

"Burgers?" she suggests.

My stomach growls in agreement. "Sounds perfect. I'll call it in while the coffee heats up. You just stay there." She hums and reclines back in the bed while I pull on my shorts.

"I could get used to this. Feel free to spoil me anytime," she admits.

After heating up the coffee, I take everything into her bedroom.

"Here you go, coffee and a Danish. Burgers should be here in forty minutes."

"Forty?" She perks up her brows with a suggestive look.

"You're insatiable."

"It's been a while."

"Oh, so is this all I'm good for? Scratching an itch?" I pout.

"Absolutely not!" She leans in to give me a kiss. "Honestly, I have never felt this way about someone so soon. I told you it's hard for me to trust, but there is just something about you that makes me confident you won't try to control me or break my heart. Which means I've been more forward with you than anyone I've ever been with."

"Thank you for telling me how you feel. I won't break your heart if you don't break mine."

"Deal!" she seals it with another kiss. "Wanna watch a show while we wait for our food? There's a cute sitcom I've been binge-watching."

"Sounds good, but you have to promise you'll watch some of my favorite mysteries with me. You owe me for *Legally Blonde*."

"What? You totally enjoyed it."

"I admit it wasn't as bad as I thought it would be."

"See, there you go. But you'll like this sitcom. It's about these guys who all work in an office together, so no sororities or fashionistas."

"That could work. You going to put some clothes on?"

"Nah, I'm fine wrapped in the sheet. Makes for easy access."

"I can't argue with that." I laugh and swat her butt as we walk out of her room to the living room. I break down the massage table and move it out of the way so we can watch the show. Ally lays her head in the crook of my shoulder and turns on the TV.

We finish a second episode while we eat lunch and then stay in bed for the rest of the weekend, minus a few water and snack breaks.

CHAPTER TWENTY-THREE

Oliver

MONDAY MORNING COMES way too fast. I'm putting on my shoes when Ally comes out of the bathroom.

"So, I'm going to do some work over at the apartment today while I'm here, but then I need to get back to writing. I like to keep a tight schedule and I'm way off."

"You shouldn't let yourself get so distracted. I mean what could you have been doing all this time that was so important?" she teases, straddling my lap.

I grab her by the waist and pull her to me and tumble us back onto the bed. "Gee, I don't know. I guess I'm just easily distracted."

"Well, I have to work and be responsible, so you should go," she bops my nose with her finger and runs away laughing.

I finish tying my shoes and meet her by the door.

"Have a good day. Call me later?" she asks.

"I will. See you." I lean down and give her a long kiss until I need to come up for air. "Bye, sweetheart."

"Bye." I hear her sigh as I walk out door.

I'M HUFFING AND puffing in bliss as I arrange Ty's gym equipment. I never thought I'd be happy doing something like this, but after the weekend I just had, I can't keep the smile off my face and the joyful tune out of my whistle.

It's nearly twelve and just as I'm about to call Ally to take her to lunch, my mom's number comes up on the caller ID.

"Hey Mom, what's up?"

"I've got a major leak in the new plumbing. Can you come help?"

"Of course, did you call the plumber?"

"Tom said to turn off the water and he'd come over when he was done with his last job of the day. Can you stop and pick up a shop vac?"

I take a deep breath to summon my patience. "I'm on my way."

I lock up Ty's apartment and head out of the city. I stop by the hardware store to get the shop vac Mom asked for as well as some rags and cleaner, just in case.

As I'm driving my mind drifts back to my amazing

weekend with Ally. The intensity of the bond between us. I've never had that with anyone before. Tracy would be mad if I messed up her hair. But with Ally it's all passion, and we just fit like puzzle pieces. I do have *several* confirmations that I was hitting all the right spots. I'm hoping it won't take long at Mom's so I can surprise her with a romantic dinner tonight. My mind continues to conjure up future plans, both in and out of bed, with Ally and before I know it, I'm pulling in Mom's driveaway.

I grab the supplies and head to the door. "It's me, Mom," I yell as I walk in with my arms full.

"I'm down here," she calls from the basement. I find my mom wringing out water from a mop. "I came down to take some measurements and found water leaking from under the shower stall," Mom explains while I unbox the shop vac.

"That sucks. Thankfully it looks like it didn't get too much of the carpet."

"Yes, thank goodness."

"When's Tom getting here?"

"I'm not sure, just whenever he's done for the day."

"He's usually pretty good. I wonder what happened."

"I have no idea. I'm sure he'll get it fixed. He's been reliable all these years."

As we're vacuuming up the water, Tom calls Mom and she lets me know that he'll be later than expected, but he'll at least look at it tonight to see what needs to be done. He recommended we leave the water off and not mess with anything until he gets there.

Can I come stay with you?" she asks, hesitantly. I stifle groan.

"Mom, I can't have distractions right now. I just outlined a new book and with helping at Ty's..." *Oh shit.* I immediately stop talking but Mom's eyes are bugged out and I know she heard what I said.

"What do you mean you're helping at Ty's? Did you just fly in from California all of a sudden?" She crosses her arms over her chest in a you-better-tell-your-mom-the-truth stance.

"Crap. Hold on." I quickly pull up Ty's number on my phone and put it on speakerphone while we wait for him to answer.

"Hey, bro, what's up?" Ty answers.

"I'm at Mom's. A pipe burst in her basement, and she needs a place to stay? Do you have any ideas?

"I take it she knows?"

"I *may* have mentioned helping you out by accident." I wince.

"Are one of you going to explain to me exactly what is going on?" Mom interjects.

"Mom, I wanted to surprise you when I got there, but I'm moving to the city," Ty explains.

"Oh, my goodness. Ty. You're coming home? I can't

believe it. I'm so happy!" Mom cries, hopping on her toes.

"Yeah, Oliver found me an apartment just a few minutes' walk from him. He's been helping me get set up. Why don't you stay there while they are fixing your house so the bigshot can have his precious quiet time to work on his latest masterpiece," Ty adds. I glare at the phone. He's not wrong. I do need quiet to work, which is why I moved out in the first place.

"You didn't have to phrase it like that," I huff.

"I know but I have too much fun teasing you."

"Did you still want me to help set up?" I ask, sarcastically.

"Nah, I got Ma now." Ty laughs.

"I'll remember you said that," I jest.

"Don't worry, honey. I'll get it all ready for you," Mom adds with a huge grin on her face.

"Thanks Mom. I'm just finishing up some loose ends here and I'll be on my way."

"I can't wait to have both my boys back together in one place again."

"I think we just made her day. She can't stop smiling," I inform Ty.

"Good. I'm glad. I'll see you guys soon."

"Bye honey," Mom says before I disconnect.

The basement is cleaned up as best it can be for the time being, so I grab the shop vac and turn to Mom,

"Let's put this stuff away and get you packed. I need to be back in the city for dinner."

"Oh?" Mom lifts an eyebrow at me.

"It's just a dinner."

"Uh, huh." She starts cleaning up, and I know that she knows I'm not telling her the whole truth. I want to enjoy this time with Ally without putting an expectation on the relationship.

Once Mom is ready, she leaves some lights on for Tom. He already has a key, since they're each other's designated emergency buddy, and can let himself in so we can get back to the city.

Mom prattles on about Ty coming and how she can't wait to see his apartment and how excited she is about us being close again as I drive us back to the city. I let her keep talking so I don't have to talk about my vague dinner plans.

Just as I'm parking my car outside Ty's building, Tom calls my mom. I can tell by the look on her face and the tone of his voice that somethings not good. I sit impatiently, waiting for Mom to fill me in.

"He's going to have to take the whole shower stall out and might have to go behind the wall, but he won't know until he removes the stall. I know you said you had plans, but he doesn't have anyone to help him move it. Can you go help him?"

"Mom." She frowns and turns her whole body toward me.

"I'm so sorry but he says there's still water on the floor and if we turned it off then something is seriously wrong." I hang my head.

"Okay. Text him that I'm on my way back. Here's Ty's key. Apartment 202. One flight up on the right." I hand her the key. She gives me a kiss on the cheek before letting herself out.

"Thank you, sweetheart."

"You're welcome. I'll call you when I know what's going on."

I make sure Mom is safely inside the building, turn on my signal light, and prepare to make a U-turn back to the house. I'm so thankful I didn't promise anything to Ally because I wouldn't want to let her down after the weekend we had. However, I want to check in with her and let her know what's happening. I press on her number in my contacts then set the phone down. As I execute the U-turn, my phone slides off the console and lands on the floor, somehow causing the Bluetooth to disconnect because the screen on my dash goes blank. Now I'm out of luck until I get back to the house. I need this day to be over.

Forty minutes later I'm pulling into the driveway and Tom is running out the door, flagging me down.

"Hey Tom, what can I help you with?" I ask as I get out of the car and follow him into the house.

"We're going to need to pull this shower stall out and see what's going on. I have the caulking all pulled up, so we should be able to just pull it out together," he explains as he leads to me to the bathroom.

Once we're in position, Tom and I each grab a side and then…*whoosh.* A wave of water comes crashing down on me.

"Crap!" It's as if I'm in a torrential rainstorm and can't see anything in front of me.

"Pull harder kid so I can get back to the pipe."

I blindly grasp for the shower stall and do as he says. Then everything happens in slow motion. I pull back. My feet slip out from under me, and I land on my back. My phone slides out of my pocket and floats out of the bathroom on the river flowing into the living area. Tom's muscling the stall to get around it and thankfully keeps it from crushing me as it toddles in place from his movements. I'm so stunned at the situation that I just stare at the water raining down and Tom stepping over me.

"I've got to get to the main water supply. I thought your mom said she turned it off," he yells over the rushing water while running to the storage area.

Lord only knows what she thought she turned off. I'm trying to get up and out of the waterfall, mimicking a baby fawn finding its legs, when it finally stops. I slip and slide my way out of the bathroom and onto the ruined carpet. To say we have a slight mess on our hands is a gross understatement.

"You okay, kiddo?" Tom asks when he returns, assessing the damage.

"I think so," I say, looking at my soaking wet clothes and hoping Mom still has a pair of my sweats for me to change into.

"You better call your mom. It's going to be a long night."

I plod through the ankle-deep water to where I think my phone might be but find it under the coffee table instead. As I pick it up, the screen flashes and turns off. *Terrific. This day is just getting better and better.*

"Tom, I've got to run upstairs and use the house phone. I think we wiped out my cell."

"I'm coming with you. I've got to get a bunch of stuff from my truck." We slosh to the stairs and leave a trail of water on the steps.

When I get to the kitchen phone there is no dial tone. *What. The. Hell.* I run back down to find that the cable box was lucky enough to be on the same wall as the broken pipe and has now had its own shower and no longer feels like working. I tug on my hair in frustration and go back upstairs to find Tom.

As he walks into the house with his hands full, I ask him for his phone. He puts down his toolbox to hand it to me then proceeds downstairs.

"Hi Tom, what did you find out?" Mom greets.

"It's me. I don't have good news for you."

"Oh no, what happened?"

"The pipe behind the shower broke. The basement is now flooded, and the cable and phone are out because the box shared the same wall as the shower and apparently doesn't like water as much as my cell phone because that is also dead."

"Oh, honey. I don't know what to say." *Do I hear a hint of a laugh?*

"Apparently, the water main wasn't turned off. I thought you said you did that."

Mom clears her throat. "I turned the one off behind the toilet so it would turn off the water to that bathroom." I hang my head and now realize what happened.

"That's just the water to the toilet."

"Oh. Sweetie, I'm so sorry." She sounds remorseful this time.

"It's okay. Tom will get it fixed. I'm going to stay here and work on getting the water out of the carpeted area. Do you still have the big fan Dad had in his workshop? And possibly an old pair of my sweats?"

"Fan is in the shed. Sweats are in your dresser."

"Thanks. Call me on Tom's phone if you need me. I won't have a phone until I can get this cleaned up."

"Thank you, sweetie. I'm sorry I caused such a mess and can't help you."

"You can help me by setting up Ty's apartment."

"That I can do!"

"Thanks."

"Thank *you*. I'll call the insurance company in the morning."

"All right. Talk to you later."

"Bye."

I grumble and stomp up the stairs to my old bedroom to get changed.

CHAPTER TWENTY-FOUR

Allison

I'M NOT SURE how I manage to get any work done after the magical weekend I've had. I missed my chance to call Morgan this morning and my leg is bouncing in eager excitement for her lunch break. I've already texted her that she MUST call me as soon as she is away from her desk.

At 12:32 my phone rings.

"Morgan!"

"Hey Ally, I'm sensing you have something you need to tell me?" Her sarcasm knows no bounds.

"How'd you know?"

"Maybe the twenty-four text messages I got gave it away," Morgan sasses.

"I just had the most amazing weekend of my life. I basically had sex for forty-eight hours." I throw my arms up in glee.

"How are you alive?"

"Okay, not forty-eight hours straight, but let's just

say, I was naked all weekend."

"Oooh, girl, I'm not even going to pretend to not be jealous. Do you think his brother is just as good?"

"Are you already planning to jump his bones the minute he gets here?"

"I might give him a day or two to settle in. Now, tell me all the details. Is he good? Big? Attentive?"

"Oh God, yes. Very. And there isn't a part of my body that hasn't been ravished."

"I hate you."

"I know. It's okay. Because I can't even believe it myself." I shrug my shoulders and smile.

"I give you a hard time but I'm one hundred percent happy for you. I'm glad you're back to your old self. Being fun and flirty and having amazing sex with a hot guy always helps!"

"Thanks, bestie. It's refreshing to feel good again. I can't tell you what it's like to be able to be myself and get fawned over."

"I think that's what we all strive for."

"I agree. And I think Oliver may be the one." I fiddle with the pen on my desk, spinning it.

"You did say you were going to marry him."

"I did? When?" I sit upright.

"When you first ran into him."

"No, I didn't. I didn't even know him then," I defend, slapping my desk in defiance.

"You did. I remember laughing at you in your stunned state."

"Well, see, there you go. I was stunned and not thinking clearly."

"Uh huh. I think you knew."

"I didn't." I protest. "Love at first sight is so over-used."

"It sounds like you used the term correctly."

"I definitely like him," I hedge.

"I can hear the tone in your voice, and I think you love him, Ally."

"Morgan."

"Let yourself go and admit it."

"We'll see," I say, coyly. "I can definitely say I'm falling for him," I admit.

"I'll let your half-assed admission slide. And, on that note, I better grab something to eat and take it back to my desk."

I disconnect and stare at my computer screen until the words blur and my stomach growls. I guess I need some lunch too. I wonder if Oliver is still here.

I cross the hall and knock but everything is quiet, no shuffling or banging, so he must have left already. I'm kinda bummed he didn't come back for another kiss before he left. I shrug and then head to the market for lunch.

When I walk in the door, I immediately scan for

Oliver since we always seemed to run into each other, but it's pretty empty. I sigh in defeat and grab a pre-made sandwich and a small bag of chips then head to the register.

"He's not here, darling," Rose informs me.

"How did you—"

"I watch and I know. So, I take it you guys are an item now?" She winks.

"Yes, very much so." I'm pretty sure I'm grinning like the Cheshire cat.

"You make a beautiful couple. It's going to last."

"I hope so. I've never felt this way about anyone before, even men I thought would be good options in the past."

"The heart knows."

"I think you're right. Thanks, Rose."

"Anytime, dear. Have a good afternoon," she says, handing me the bag with my items.

When I return home, I try to call Oliver and it goes straight to voicemail. Huh, that's super weird. I continue to work the rest of the day since I didn't get much done this morning and then try to call him again to meet for dinner. Still nothing. I'm trying not to worry, but what's up? He doesn't seem like the type of guy who would use a woman for sex, so now all the bad thoughts are running through my head. Is he lying on the floor across the hall under some heavy-weight machine? Did he get hit by a car going home? Did someone put a gun to his head and tell him to write his book and he wasn't allowed to call anyone until his pages were done?

I shake the crazy thoughts out of my head as I reach for the peanut butter swirl ice cream I have stashed in the back of my fridge, grab a spoon, and plop on the couch before calling Morgan.

"Hey Ally, what's up?"

"I can't get ahold of Oliver. His phone has been going to voicemail all day, and I'm starting to get worried."

"If he wham-bam-thank-you-ma'amed you, he better run."

"Morgan, why would you say that? I'm thinking he's in a ditch somewhere and now you put that in my head. He wouldn't."

"I'm sorry. I'm sure he didn't. Did you ever stop to think that his battery is dead?"

"All day? Come on."

"I know. I'm just trying to think of a rational explanation. Can you go to his place?"

I cringe. "I don't actually know where he lives. He always comes here."

"That's out. Hmm, email?"

"Nope."

"Publisher?"

"Oh yes, 'Hello super busy person, could you tell me how to find my new boyfriend?' That would go over well."

"I'm sure he's fine. Did he say where he was going after he left this morning?"

"Just across the hall to set up and then to write."

"Ally. Duh, he probably turned his phone off to write and not be distracted." I drop my spoon.

"Morgan you're a genius. That's it! I did think of a scenario where he had a gun to his head to write all the words, but this is more rational. Just a simple 'do not disturb.' Thank you!"

"I know. And you're welcome. Now stop eating that ice cream and stop worrying."

"How did you know?"

"I'm not new here. Look, just relax and I'm sure he'll call you tomorrow."

"I'm putting the ice cream away as we speak. Thank you for saving my stomach a night of discomfort."

"Anytime. Bye, babe."

After closing the freezer, I do my nightly rounds of running the dishwasher and turning off all the lights, then make my way to bed. I lean down and inhale the scent of the peonies and grab Oliver's book while admonishing myself for thinking the worst as I get into bed.

When I flip open the cover, I realize Oliver signed it and wrote an inscription. It reads: *To the woman I'd hide a body for.* I laugh and hug the book to my chest realizing just how ridiculous I've been.

CHAPTER TWENTY-FIVE
Allison

WHEN I WAKE up with Oliver's book nestled in my arms, I'm still in a funk from not having heard from him. After I get ready for the day, I bury myself in my work to get him off my mind. I'm just getting off one call when a new one comes in.

"Hello, Moore Than Words, how can I help you?"

"Good afternoon, cutie."

"Hey, handsome. I was on the other line and didn't recognize the number. How are you today?"

"Terrific. I called because I want to rearrange the products page to show that I'm offering some new workouts. I've got a lot of people now interested in Zoom classes that I need to add to the navigation."

"That's awesome. You could be anywhere and still work out. I like that."

"Are you going to join one of my classes now?"

"The first time you see me will not be all sweaty in workout gear."

"And what would you be wearing on our first date?" *Is he flirting with me?*

"What?" I ask, unsure of how he means this comment.

"I wanted to know what you wear on first dates. Do you get dressed up or like to stay casual? You know, for when I come to New York and take you to dinner." I almost took his comment the wrong way. He just wants to take me out for a friendly meal.

"I'd say, somewhere I could wear a nice dress but not too formal. Since I work from home I like to dress up once in a while."

"I'll make a note of that," he says.

"When are you coming?" I ask.

"It might be sooner than I expected from when we talked about it last time, but maybe I'll surprise you."

"I think I'd rather know."

"You don't like surprises?"

"Not exactly."

"I wouldn't want to make you uncomfortable. You've become a good friend as well as a business connection and I'd like to take you out when I'm in town for all the hard work you've done. You may have talked me off some relationship ledges as well." I swear I can almost hear him wink through the phone. *See, just a friendly meal. He's not flirting.*

"Yeah, of course. I'd like that. Is there anyone new yet?"

"I appreciate that you think I work that quickly, but no, I'm too busy with the business right now. Hopefully, I'll find someone when things settle down."

"I don't doubt it. Look, I've got to run. I'll work on your changes this week. Shouldn't take too long."

"Thank you, Allison. I'll email you the details. Have a great rest of the day."

"You too, Grant."

I know, I know, I know. I should have told him I have a boyfriend. But technically he was only asking me to a business dinner.

One day of no communication from Oliver doesn't mean we're over, right? I can't allow myself to think the worst. But what does it mean? It doesn't give me warm fuzzies that he hasn't called me since having sex. He was all about spoiling me and calling me sweetheart. He wouldn't ditch me, would he? Ugh, seriously, why can't there be an Angi's List for guys?

I know Morgan can't talk so I text her.

Ally: OMG. Grant is really coming to NY!

Morgan: OMG. When?

Ally: He said soon. Before it was a few weeks. Now it's soon!

Morgan: Be careful.

Ally: It's just a business dinner.

Morgan: Is it?

Ally: *I know I've had a crush on him, but I promised Oliver I wouldn't hurt him, and I won't make any decisions until I've heard from him.*

Morgan: *Okay. Good. Let me know when you hear from him.*

Ally: *Will do.*

I try Oliver's number again and it goes straight to voicemail…again. I decide to text him.

Ally: *Hey, I wish you were here.*

I'm shocked when I get an immediate response.

Handsome: *Me too.*

Ally: *We could order dinner and you could give me a massage…*

Handsome: *Wow. I'm surprised.*

Ally: *Why? We have great chemistry together. Can't you feel it?*

Handsome: *Yes, I thought so, but I didn't want to scare you off.*

Ally: *You could never. When can you come over?*

Handsome: *Soon…*

Soon? What the hell does that mean? I scream at the ceiling and then look back down at my phone.

Oh…My…God…I have to call him immediately.

"Grant! I am so so sorry. I wasn't trying to be unprofessional. Please disregard those texts!" I shout out in one breath when he answers the phone.

"I have to say, I kind of liked them. I always felt like we had a connection and I wanted to take you to dinner to see if something would come of it."

"We do, but I'm sorta seeing someone."

"I *think* you would know if you were seeing someone."

"Well, I was—am—and we uh, you know, and now he's ghosting me. I was sending those texts to see if I could get him to respond since my calls are going to voicemail."

"Ouch. You want to be with someone who calls and follows up, especially to texts like that. I definitely wouldn't ghost you. You deserve better than that."

"Thank you."

"Hopefully there's a good reason he hasn't called, but if it doesn't work out with him, maybe I can convince you to give me a try."

"You haven't even met me yet."

"But we've known each other for almost five years. I know you more than you think I do."

"That's sweet, but I need to give this new guy a chance."

"As you wish," Grant relents.

"Thank you. I'll let you know when the updates are done."

"And I'll let you know when I'm coming."

"Can't wait."

I hang up and immediately feel better. Grant is a great guy and I'm so glad he didn't fire me on the spot. I have more pep in my step and log onto his website to make the updates he's requested with a huge smile on my face.

CHAPTER TWENTY-SIX

Oliver

TOM AND I worked through the night and I'm exhausted. While he fixed the pipe, I vacuumed up the water with the shop vac. Let me tell you that I seriously underestimated the size I needed because after a thousand trips out of the basement door to dump the water, my back may be in need of chiropractic assistance. Once the furniture and water were out of the way I pulled up the carpet to find that even the concrete was damp from the fiasco. Fans are fanning to help dry things out and I'm sitting at the kitchen table waiting for the insurance adjuster to come look at the damage.

I'm having a hard time sitting still. I don't have my computer, so I can't work or email anyone. I don't have Ally's number because my dead phone is holding it hostage—I knew I should have written it down—and as much as I'm eager to let her know that I'm not dead or blowing her off, I'm severely hesitant to send Mom over to fill her in.

I'm not ready to share her with the family. I want us to have time for the lightness and fun of a new relationship. If Mom goes over there, the wedding will be planned and there will be talk of grandchildren.

I'm brought out of my thoughts when there's a knock at the door. I let in the adjuster and lead him to the waterlogged realm. I explain the events of the night before as he looks over the entire basement. The adjuster informs me that he'll submit his findings to the insurance company and Mom will get an email with all the information she needs to get the cleanup process started. I thank him and walk him to the door.

When I return to the kitchen, I realize it's gotten late. I can't call Mom or Ally with an update without a phone, so I grab my keys and head to the store to get a new cell phone.

"Welcome to Verizon. I'm Christina, how may we help you?" A petite brunette with a kind smile greets me as I enter the store.

"My phone is water-damaged, and I need to get a new one and transfer all my data."

"Sure thing. We don't have a wait, so follow me. Do you plan to upgrade or just replace?"

"Might as well upgrade."

"Just pick out the phone you'd like and meet me at the second desk along the back wall."

"Thank you."

I decide to get the newest model of an iPhone in black and meet her at the desk.

"If you give me your phone number, I can bring up your account."

I give her my number and we confirm that I am eligible for an upgrade and that they do have the new phone in stock. She takes my old phone, inspects it, then confirms it is in fact dead from water damage and that she'll have to get all my info from the cloud to transfer.

"When was the last time you backed up to the cloud?"

"Uh, I don't remember. I thought I had set it to automatically backup because I knew I'd forget to do it."

"Okay then, we should have it all up and running in a few minutes. Let me get your new phone. I'll be right back."

As I'm waiting, I hear someone call my name and the hairs on the back of my head stand on end. It's…my ex.

"Tracy."

"Oliver. It's so good to see you." She leans in for a hug, but I step back and she stumbles but quickly corrects her footing.

"Huh, you didn't seem like you were going to miss me all that much when you canceled our wedding." She swats my arm.

"Ooooh, don't hold a grudge, Oliver. It will make you old before your time. I'd love to get some coffee with you and catch up."

I straighten my back and look down at her. "I don't think that would be a good idea. I'm seeing someone."

"So am I. It would be a purely innocent, old-friends meet up."

"I don't have anything to say to you. I'm sorry but I'll pass. If you'll excuse me, I need to get back to this," I say, gesturing to Christina who has returned to her desk and is unboxing the new phone.

Tracy huffs. "Fine. I was just trying to be nice. Now, I'm even more confident that I made the right decision. I better go catch up with my new *fiancé*. Later, Olly."

She abruptly turns on her heel and wraps her arm through some guy's as she approaches the door and storms out.

"Wow, I don't mean to get into your personal business but you totally dodged a bullet there."

"Yeah."

"Well, if it doesn't work out with your current girl-friend, you have my number." Christina winks and continues the transfer process.

I huff out a laugh and thank her. She has me pay for the phone and then starts the download process. I fidget with the seam on my pant leg while I wait. It's amazing how much we rely on our phones to keep us entertained.

"Okay, Oliver. I have pulled all the info you had backed up from the cloud and you should be good to go."

"Thank you."

"You're welcome. Please let me know if there is anything else I can help you with."

I scroll through my photos and contacts and am happy to see everything is there…except…hold on…Ally's number is missing. *Shit.* I hang my head in frustration, and when I look up, Christina is looking at me with concern.

"I'm missing some numbers," I explain.

"If it's newer information, it's possible it was entered after the last backup."

"Thanks. I've gotta run. I appreciate all your help."

"I'm here any time." She winks again and waves goodbye.

When I get into my car, I hook up the new phone to the Bluetooth and call Mom.

"Hi, honey."

"Hi. I'm on my way home to get some rest but then I'll come by Ty's in the morning."

"I don't think so."

"What? Why?"

"I need you back at my place to meet with the cable guy," she responds, and I bang my head on the steering wheel.

"Mom."

"I'm sorry."

"Fine. At least I can get some work done while I

wait."

"Thank you. You know I appreciate all you've done for me."

"It's okay. I'll talk to you tomorrow."

I drive home and crash into bed, hoping I can dream of Ally if I can't talk to her.

CHAPTER TWENTY-SEVEN
Allison

I CAN'T BELIEVE I managed to keep my mind off Oliver for the rest of the afternoon. I'm just about done for the day when I get a call from an unknown number. I find that it's a new client looking for website services and take down all their information. After hanging up with them, I hear knocking on my door. I jump out of my chair and run to the door hoping it's Oliver. When I look out the peephole, I see an older woman standing there and open the door.

"Hello?" I say tentatively.

"Hi, I'm Ellen Hudson. My son is moving in across the hall and I'm here setting up the place for him. Do you happen to have any cleaners and paper towels I could use? I'll replace them tomorrow. I didn't realize it had gotten so late, and I'm not comfortable walking to the market in the dark," Ellen rattles off an explanation. She's a tall brunette woman with some grey at her temples and sparkling hazel eyes.

My face softens as I realize I'm meeting Oliver's mother for the first time and she has no idea who I am.

"Hi, Ellen. I'm Ally. As a matter of fact, I do. Come in and I'll get them for you."

"Thank you," she says as she walks in and looks around my place. "You have a lovely home. Do you know I can help you get that stain out of your carpet." *How can she see it? I know where it is, and I can barely make it out.*

"Darn, I thought we did a good job getting the stain out," I say, joining her, staring at the spot.

"I'm guessing red wine?" She tsks.

"It was. Wow, are you a spot guru?" I ask in awe.

"No, I just raised two boys and had to become a stain expert. I know it's a set stain, but I'll mix up my secret stain remover and get the rest out."

"That would be great. I can barely see it anymore, but it will be nice to have it out completely. Thank you."

"No problem." She pats my arm. "I'll let you get back to whatever you were doing. Thank you for the cleaning products."

"You're welcome. Feel free to knock any time. I work from home, so I'm here if you need anything."

"Thank you. It's so nice to know I'm not alone here."

"Have a good evening," I say before closing the door.

As soon as she leaves, I grab my phone and text Morgan.

Ally: *Guess who I just met?*

Morgan: *Who?*

Ally: *Oliver's mother!*

Morgan: *What? When? How did you know it was her?*

Ally: *My new neighbor's mother came over to borrow cleaning supplies.*

Morgan: *Did you tell her who you were?*

Ally: *No, and I'm going to befriend her and find out what's going on with Oliver.*

Morgan: *OMG! That's slick!*

Ally: *Thanks. I'm thinking bagels and coffee in the morning.*

Morgan: *Oooh, I like the way you think.*

Ally: *I'll let you know what I find out.*

Morgan: *You better. Talk later.*

Ally: *Later.*

I dance around in excitement at my new spy mission then plop on my couch to watch a show before bed.

CHAPTER TWENTY-EIGHT

Allison

FIRST THING IN the morning, I run to the market and grab some bagels, cream cheese, and juice for my welcome chat with Ellen. When I get back to the building I go straight to the door across the hall from mine and knock.

"Good morning, Ellen," I greet when she answers, lifting the grocery bag. "I brought you some breakfast."

"How nice of you. I was just getting ready to run out myself, but now I'll have breakfast first. Would you like some coffee?"

"Yes, thank you." As she's fixing the coffee, I take a look around. Lots of sunlight comes in from the large windows. The hardwood floor shines from a recent cleaning and all the gym equipment is neatly lined up along the far wall with all the weights and bands neatly stacked on the opposite wall. The kitchen sparkles from the elbow grease only a mother can provide, and it smells clean and fresh. "Wow, everything looks amazing. You've done a lot of work."

"Thank you. My other son set up the weight equipment, and I did the kitchen. Now to tackle the bedrooms. I'll work on those today."

"Speaking of your other son…his name wouldn't happen to be Oliver, would it?"

"Yes, have you met him?" I blush because I most certainly have met him.

"Yes. We've run into each other a couple of times at the market, and he mentioned his brother was moving into my building." *What? I didn't lie.*

"Oh, that's great. It will be so nice for Ty to already have a friendly face living across the hall when he gets here."

"I'd be happy to welcome him to the building and show him around."

"He's been in California for a few years so it might be nice for him to get used to the area again."

"Are he and Oliver alike?"

"In more ways than one. I just hope they act like the gentlemen I raised them to be when they're around you."

"Oliver did seem nice and did treat me to some dinners," I say, hoping to slide the conversation toward Oliver's dating patterns.

"That's nice of him." She looks me up and down. "Are you sure they weren't dates? That boy falls hard, and you look just like his type." I blush.

"You caught me. He took me to Martino's. We had a great time."

"Martino's?" she asks, looking shocked. I'm not sure why and decide to press on. I've got to find out what is up.

"Yeah, but uh, I haven't heard from him in a few days. Do you know where he is?" I fiddle with my hands.

"Unfortunately, he's been at my house. A pipe broke in my basement while I was remodeling the bathroom and he's been helping my plumber get it fixed. It's been a big mess. He lost his phone in the water. I have no phone or cable." She waves her hands around and then pours the coffee. "My house is a wreck, and the poor thing hasn't come up for air trying to help me. Now he's there waiting for the cable company to come put in new equipment." She sighs and takes a sip of her coffee.

OMG…no wonder I couldn't get a hold of him. Now I feel bad that I thought the worst when he's been a doting son.

"Wow. That's a lot. I'm sorry to hear that happened."

"It's not ideal. But at least I'm here helping set up Ty's apartment so I can be useful."

"You can put me to work too. I'm here to help."

"Thank you. Why don't you start on the bathrooms. Would you mind wiping everything down with cleanser while I find the linen boxes?"

"Whatever you need."

"Great. And we also need good music." She turns on some classic rock and we get to work.

By the end of the day, we are sweaty and dirty, but only a few boxes remain in the spare bedroom. They are full of decorations that Ellen decided Ty should put up where he wants.

"Let me know if you need anything else. I have a few projects to work on, but I'll be around if you need me," I tell her as I make my way to the door.

"Thank you, Ally. It was a great day."

"It was. I enjoyed hearing all the stories about Oliver and Ty. They remind me of my brothers."

"They're all the same when they're teenagers. Now, I can enjoy myself and not worry about them quite as much."

"Speaking of time for yourself, my friend Morgan and I have monthly bar crawls. Would you like to join us?"

"I would love that."

"Great. The next one is next Saturday. Will you still be here?"

"Yes, it's all going to take a while to fix."

"Okay, it starts at nine p.m. and you can go to as many as you want, but we always end up at Finnegan's around the corner.

"Thank you for the invite. Are you sure you don't

mind a mom tagging along?"

"Are you kidding? No way. You've got it going on."

"True." She struts and poses for emphasis, and we both laugh.

"You'll fit right in," I say.

"Sounds fun. Thank you."

"You're welcome. I'll see you later."

I WALK BACK to my apartment, strip off my clothes, and take an insanely long shower to wash away the sweat and grim. Ellen is amazing, and I can see why Oliver is such a great guy.

CHAPTER TWENTY-NINE
Oliver

AFTER A RESTFUL night's sleep, my brain can function again. I'm at Mom's with a coffee, my laptop, and my new phone. I can now think clearly. I use my phone as a hub and log on to the internet to find Ally's work number, which should also be her cell phone number.

I dial and get her voicemail, so I send an email to her work as well letting her know what's been going on and how sorry I am that I haven't been available to her after the weekend we had and how I can't wait to make it up to her. In a more eloquent, I actually *do* know how to write, way. One that I hope will make it easy for her to forgive me.

After seeing Tracy, I realized that Ally is nothing like her and it makes me want to be with her even more. For a while there, I thought it was me. That I put too much pressure on the relationship. But, after seeing her and knowing that she only asked me to coffee to gloat about her *new fiancé,* I know that she did me a favor by canceling the wedding.

I wipe away all thoughts of Tracy and temporarily store thoughts of Ally to get some writing done. By lunchtime, I still haven't gotten a call from the cable guy, so I make a quick dash to grab some lunch and get back.

By three I'm annoyed and call Mom.

"Hi, honey."

"Hey, have you heard from the cable people? I haven't, and they are way past their service window."

"Hang on, let me put you on speakerphone and see if I have a message. I might have been vacuuming when they called."

We get disconnected. She calls back.

"Sorry, you know me and phones. They left a message saying they have to come tomorrow." *I love my mom. I love my mom.* I chant in my head to keep my cool.

"I'll lock up and head home then."

"You don't want to come here for dinner? Maybe ask Ally if she'd like to join us?"

"How do you know about Ally?"

"The question is why didn't you tell me that you were dating your brother's neighbor?"

"Umm…" I can't think of a lie fast enough.

"You didn't want me finding out about her, did you?"

"It's not like that. We just started seeing each other, and I didn't want to say anything too soon."

"The mother is always the last to know."

"She is when she threatens to talk to every girl you meet about weddings on the first date."

"I do no such thing."

"Mom."

"Oliver."

"Okay, not the first date," I concede and then continue. "Look, I really like her and don't want to screw this up."

"She was worried about you and asked if I knew where you were. Don't worry, I explained everything. She seemed to relax after that and then helped me clean the rest of Ty's apartment."

"See, isn't she great?"

"Yes, so don't screw it up."

I groan. "I'm not trying to. That's why I need to get some of this stuff done so I can spend time with her."

"Now that your phone is working you should give her a call. She's a great girl and was willing to help clean your brother's place. She'll understand."

"I tried but it went to voicemail, and I also sent a very nice email explaining everything."

"Good. Drive safe and I'll see you tomorrow."

I end the call and yell out in frustration. I can't believe she met Ally before I could introduce them. This whole remodel has been an albatross around my love life. I need to get to Ally. When I get in the car, I call her again. Straight to voicemail. I'm so frustrated I bang on the steering wheel and yell some more. This can't be happening. I need to get to her, and I have to come back here tomorrow. I just hope she even speaks to me when I finally get to see her.

CHAPTER THIRTY
Allison

I GENUINELY WANTED to help Ellen with Ty's apartment yesterday, but I also wanted to get the scoop on Oliver. That might not have been the best plan because today I'm going crazy. I have four different projects in different stages and none of them are going well because my mind is constantly drifting to Oliver. I miss him so much, but I know he had to take care of his mom's stuff. Then there's Grant, who just admitted after five years that he wouldn't mind if our business dinner turned into a social event. And on top of it all, I have the bar crawl to finalize. Or maybe three bars are good enough and I can be done. Then there's Ellen, Oliver's nice mother who is bar hopping with us. *Can you say, cluster???*

I'm currently staring at the email I'm sending out to the Pub Crawlers group letting them know the charity we picked, lung cancer, with a photo of the gray shirt with neon paint spots splashed on it. We're starting at a black light bar to show off the shirts and then we'll end up at Finnegan's. I also mention that if anyone wants to pitch in and pick more bars, I'd appreciate it since I'm swamped and moody, but I don't type the moody part. Then I hit send and decide I need some yoga time.

Just as I roll out the mat, I hear knocking on the door across the hall and check the peephole.

"Mom, open up. I'm here." *Oliver!*

My heart takes over and I swing the door wide open and then run and jump on Oliver's back. I smother his cheek with kisses and progress down his neck before nuzzling my nose into his shoulder. *Did he start using new cologne?*

"I missed you so much."

"Uh, hello." I drop down to my feet, and he turns, revealing a bewildered look.

"What's with the face, Oliver? Didn't you miss me?"

"Oh," he starts to laugh. "You must be Ally." He holds out his hand for me to shake but I slap it away.

"Oliver, I know we haven't seen each other in a while, but you don't have to act like you don't know me." I put my hand on my hip and stomp my foot with a pout.

Just then the door in front of us opens and Ellen squeals. "Ty! You're home early!" He turns and hugs Ellen while I mentally dial the number for rent-a-forklift to help me pick my jaw up off the floor.

"Ty, I see you met Ally," Ellen says. "Ally, this is Ty." Now that I really look at him, the only differences I see are the tan and extra muscles. Everything else is Oliver staring back at me.

I cover my mouth with my hand and shake my head as I look him up and down, and Ellen laughs from behind him.

"I take it Oliver didn't mention he had an identical twin."

I remove my hand from my face. "No, he said brother but never said twin. Oh my gosh, I could die right now. I'm so sorry I jumped you."

"I have to say it was quite a greeting. I just wish you weren't already taken." I blush.

"Stop flirting with your brother's girlfriend," Ellen admonishes and slaps him on the shoulder. *Girlfriend?*

"Ouch." Ty shrugs his shoulder out of the way. "It was nice to meet you, Ally."

"Nice to meet you too," I say, trying not to gawk.

Ty turns back to his mom, and they walk into his apartment. I hang back, not sure I'm invited but they didn't close the door, so I'm guessing it's okay to follow them in.

"You cleaned! It looks so good in here."

"Yes, your apartment is almost ready for clients."

"Mom, you're awesome. Thank you so much." Ty scoops Ellen up in his arms and swings her around.

"You're letting me live with you while the basement gets fixed, so I figured I'd earn my keep. Ally helped too."

"What?" He spins around and looks at me. "No you didn't." He shakes his head in disbelief.

"Yep!"

"Wow, that was generous of you. I'm glad Oliver found this place. I think I already like my new neighbor." I blush because I can't form thoughts on what I'm feeling right now since I miss Oliver, and yet a guy who looks like Oliver is standing right here, and it's all messing with my head.

"Me too. Now it will be easy to see all of you when I come to visit," Ellen says.

"Let me drop my bags and take you both to dinner as a thank you."

"I like the sound of that! I'll go get dressed," I say before hurrying into my apartment.

"I'm going to take a quick shower and then I'll come get you," Ty says from his doorway.

"I'm going to change too," Ellen adds from behind him before I shut my door.

I take a quick shower, not washing my hair because I decide to curl it before dinner, and then finish getting ready just in time for Ellen and Ty to be knocking at my door.

"Hey, guys. Perfect timing. I'm all ready. Where are

we off too?"

"Martino's?" Ty asks.

"That was your father's and my favorite restaurant," Ellen says.

"I know. Is it okay if we go?"

"I would love to go and share a meal with you two. I just wish Oliver could join us."

"Oh shit, I should have called him and told him I'm here early."

"It's okay. He said he had writing to do since he's behind from helping out at the house. It will give us time to catch up, and you can get to know Ally," Ellen says, giving me a look. I feel like she knows something but doesn't want to betray Oliver's trust.

Ty holds out his arms, and Ellen and I link our elbows with his as we walk out to the curb and hail a cab.

CHAPTER THIRTY-ONE
Allison

MORGAN AND I missed our morning call because she had an early staff meeting, so I'm sitting at my kitchen table eating a salad for lunch while we talk.

"Ty is Oliver's *twin*?" Morgan gasps. "Yippee, I'm so jumping his bones!"

"Morgan!"

"What? I totally called dibs before I even knew what he looked like, and since he's as hot as Oliver, now I definitely want in on the action."

"He *is* pretty awesome. I had the best night with him and Ellen. He took us to Martino's as a thank you for helping set up his apartment. We laughed so much my sides hurt. Then Ellen told us stories about when her husband used to take her there for special occasions. Now I know why Oliver picked it for our first official date." I choke out the last part.

"Are you okay?"

"I just miss him. I jumped Ty thinking he was Oliver

for goodness' sake," I giggle, forking a crouton.

"See, you're totally falling for Oliver. And you're going to fix me up with Ty."

"Is that the only reason you want me to make up with Oliver?"

"You know me better than that. I want you to be happy, and Oliver makes you happy."

"Until he ghosted me."

"Do I need to come over there and kick you in the bahooty? You're being ridiculous. His mom told you what happened."

"I know, but, hello, there are moments in the day when he could have called. I mean, he couldn't have called before he went to bed? This all comes back to me waiting on a guy again. So why would I call him? It would be his responsibility to call me. He should be the one calling to explain. I could have helped him. And, if he's the type of guy who doesn't want my help, why have me in his life? I'm not waiting around to be told when to be there and when not to be again. I'm done with that."

"I personally think you're making more of this than it is, but I do see how you could feel that way."

"Was that so hard to admit? You're always supposed to see it my way."

"We can't always get over past hurts," she says.

"You know who hasn't hurt me?"

"Don't say it. Do not say his name," Morgan warns

sternly.

"Grant."

"You said it." She sighs.

"He admitted he wanted to see if there was something between us. Maybe I should give him a chance before I make any decisions."

"Ally, imagine I'm standing in front of you holding your shoulders so I don't wring your neck. Listen to me good. You are a strong, independent woman. You are not a lovestruck teenager. Grant is a client. Oliver is probably trying to keep you out of this mess, and you can't jump ship. You need to call him and get to the bottom of this like a mature adult." I wiggle in my chair in discomfort. I know I'm being ridiculous. I heave a big sigh and sit upright.

"You're right. Let me get back to work, and then I'll figure what I'm going to do."

"I know I'm right. Now go."

"Bye, Morgan," I sing into the phone with a knowing tone.

I disconnect and throw myself into my work when I notice the bright sunlight has turned to orange and the golden hour has settled in. I stare out my window and meditate on the last few days and Oliver. I've enjoyed getting to know Ellen, but Oliver hasn't texted, and my heart is flippy-floppy.

A notification ping sounds on my computer letting

me know I have a new email, bringing me back to reality. It's from Grant asking about the updates. *I swear I did those right away.* I quickly check his site and realize it never updated. I decide to call him.

"Hey, cutie," he answers.

"Oh, whew, thank you for not being mad at me. I did the work but forgot to update. I just refreshed your page, so it should be all set up."

"I could never be mad at you. Plus, you might be mad at me."

"Why is that? You didn't decide to go with another company did you?"

"No way. I just need one last update. Remember when I said I'd tell you when I was coming to take you to dinner?"

"Of course!"

"Well, I'm not just coming to visit. I've officially moved to New York and need to update my bio and address."

"Oh my gosh, that's awesome!"

"I know. Now, when and where can I take you to dinner?"

"I have our monthly bar crawl Saturday, so maybe next weekend?"

"You can't see my face, but I'm pouting. Don't I get an invitation to the crawl? I mean, don't you want to help me get to know people? And didn't you say that there were a bunch of girls in your group?"

"That there definitely is." I smile.

"Great. What time Saturday?"

"Nine. We're all meeting at Loco Larry's on Ludlow."

"Great. I'll meet you there."

"Wait. How am I going to know who you are?"

"I'm pretty sure the tan and muscles will give me away." *Well, hello Mr. Cocky.*

"What, you don't think we have personal trainers here?"

"No, but it's November and you East Coasters are probably pretty pale by now."

"You don't know, a lot of people could use tanning beds here." Grant laughs.

"Don't worry, I'll find you, Allison. See ya."

Grant disconnects and I throw my phone. Men drive me nuts with their cockiness. Maybe I should become a nun and never have to deal with them again. My stomach growls so I retrieve my phone and decide to get some dinner at the market.

When I step out into the hallway, I notice the door is cracked open across the hall. I figure I'll go ask Ellen if she and Ty need anything. I gently knock on the door, but I can hear Ty talking and it sounds more formal like he's on a work call. I wait and when he ends the call, I knock again.

"Hey, Ally, what's up?" Ty asks, opening the door wider.

"Hey, Ty. I was on my way to the market to get some dinner. Did you or Ellen need anything?" I ask, looking around for Ellen.

"Mom's out with friends but I could eat. I haven't had a chance to stock up yet. Hang on, let me grab my key."

Ty walks back into his apartment to get the key and then I hear his phone ring as he walks back out.

"Sorry. Work call. I gotta take this," he says, holding up his phone while he pulls his door shut. I signal with a go-ahead wave and he answers. "Granite Fitness. This is Grant." My eyes go wide, my jaw hits the floor.

"You're Grant!"

"Allison?"

My foot slides off the top step and suddenly I'm tumbling down the stairs. What. *Ouch.* The. *Ouch.* *Ouch. Ouch…*

"Oh shit. Allison, are you okay?" Ty, Grant, whoever he is, is leaning over me and I'm seeing two of him.

"Ouwiee!" I yell out.

"What's hurt? Is your head all right?" He feels around. "Oh, you're getting a big goose egg back there.

"It hurts like a bitch, and so does the rest of me," I grunt as Ty becomes one again.

"I see your sense of humor is still intact." He huffs.

"Can you move your legs?"

"Yes."

"Arms?"

"Yes."

"Does anything feel broken?"

"No. Can you just help me up and stop asking questions?" He laughs again but I don't see what is so funny at all.

"Sure, I'm going to pick you up and carry you up the stairs. Are you okay with that?"

"Yes."

"Okay, here we go." He lifts me like I weigh two ounces and cradles me against his body. I feel so good against him as all the stinging sensations from the bruises subside.

"Do you have your key?" Ty asks when we get to my door.

"Pocket."

"Can you reach it?"

"Yeah, I have to shift."

"It's okay, I got you." I shift and extract my key from my pocket. He moves me closer to the door so I can unlock it and he carries me into my apartment.

"Which way to your bedroom?"

"That's a little forward. I don't think I'm up for that tonight."

"Would you be serious for a minute," Ty huffs.

"Straight back, first door on the left."

"I'm glad your brain is okay, but I'm trying to get you to your bed to lay down so I can get you some ice."

"I may need a few bags."

"Don't worry, I've got you. Now lay here and don't move." He holds out his hands in a stay position and backs out of my bedroom door.

"That won't be hard because it hurts to do pretty much anything."

"Okay, I'll be right back."

My head and limbs are throbbing. When I try to lay on my side, I'm pretty sure there's a huge bruise blooming because blinding stars erupt behind my eyelids and I quickly roll once more to my back. Ty returns with five sandwich bags full of ice and some hand towels.

"Here you go. Now, show me where to put these." I point to the spots, and he gently lays the bags of ice on me and one on the back of my head. "Now, I'm going to stay here and make sure you don't have a concussion." As soon as he says the word, I roll over and vomit on the floor then roll back onto my back. "Hmm, I think you just might. Okay, I'm going to have to get you cleaned up. Can you point me to towels and clean clothes?"

"Towels are in the hall closet and clothes are in my dresser. But your mom took my cleaning supplies," I moan out over the bad taste in my mouth.

"I'll be right back." A few minutes later, Ty is back

with supplies. He cleans me up first and gives me some water to swish out my mouth with and a bucket to spit into. "Okay, we have to take off your shirt, are you okay with me helping you with that?" I nod. I'm in too much pain to worry about him seeing me in my bra and hoping it's one of my sexy ones. He slowly adjusts me to a sitting position then removes my shirt and quickly pulls a shirt back over my head and covers me up. It was almost like those magic tricks where they are so fast, they can whip the tablecloth out from under the dishes.

"Whoa, can you help me get dressed every day?" I say in amazement.

"I brought you one of my shirts so I could cover you up faster."

"Thank you." I sway toward his face wanting to kiss him for his kindness but quickly remember he's not Oliver, and then I start to cry.

"You're welcome. Hey, why are you crying? Did I hurt you?"

I shake my head, but then realize that was a bad idea and cry harder.

"You're being so sweet, and everything hurts, but I want Oliver." I want to snuggle into his gentle touch so he can make all the pain go away.

"I know. He can't be here right now, but I'm here, and as soon as we can get you settled, I'll call him. Okay?"

"I nod my head gently and lay back."

"I'm going to reapply your ice packs. Ready?"

"Yes." They hurt and then start to numb the pain and bring relief as I close my eyes.

"I left you some water and after I'm done cleaning your carpet, I'll call Oliver."

"Okay, thank you, Ty. Hey, wait a minute." I pop my eyes open and try to sit up, but Ty holds me down.

"Shh, don't talk. Just rest." I'm too sore to argue and close my eyes again, quickly falling into a deep sleep.

CHAPTER THIRTY-TWO

Oliver

TY AND MY mom have tried to call me numerous times and I can't for the life of me understand why I didn't hear the ringer. It's on and turned up. I don't know what's going on with my luck lately. This new phone better not be a lemon. But I can't worry about them now. I've already got too much on my plate. Ty and Mom will just have to deal with whatever is happening over at his place.

At least I've been able to get some writing done at Mom's while waiting for the cable guy to get here. Why can't they show up when they are supposed to? I understand emergencies, but we're on day two here. Just as I'm complaining to myself, the doorbell rings and I let in the serviceman. After I show him the cable box, I leave him to work and try to call Ally. Again, it goes straight to voicemail. She's probably thinking the worst and refusing my calls. Like, how could we have an amazingly sexy weekend and then I never call her. I know Mom finally told her what happened, but I should have been the one to tell her.

The guy comes up from the basement and lets me know he has to order a new box. *Did they not tell him what I told them and how it was water-logged?* I don't ask because it won't help. He lets me know he should be able to come back next week and they'll call with a date and time frame. I thank him and show him out. Hopefully, Mom will be moved back in and I won't have to be here for that. And now that he's done early, I can *finally* go see my girl.

She needs to know I love her and how special she is to me. Being away from her has been excruciating. I didn't think I'd miss someone so much in such a short period of time. I hope she got my messages letting her know I'd see her soon. But not before picking up a bouquet of all-red peonies, hoping they mean the same thing as red roses.

Bounding up the stairs of her apartment building two at a time while whistling a tune we heard on our date at Martino's, I'm filled with excitement and can't seem to hop the steps fast enough. I knock and listen for the patter of her feet on the hardwood in her hallway. Nothing. I knock again. Still nothing. I decide to go over to Ty's apartment to see if she's there with Mom. No answer. Huh, that's weird. I try Ally's door one more time and realize that the door is unlocked. That's not normal. I let myself in, hoping she's okay. I gently lay the flowers on the kitchen table and tiptoe through the apartment, checking each room until only the bedroom is left. When I open her door to investigate, I can't believe my eyes. Ty is not only here and didn't tell me, but Ally is snuggled up next to him, wearing his college T-shirt, his favorite T-shirt that he only lets special girls wear. I walk backward out of the room and shut the door. I storm out the front door and slam it behind me. I could give a rat's ass if I wake them up.

CHAPTER THIRTY-THREE
Allison

I'M STARTLED AWAKE by the slamming of a door and shoot up into a sitting position. Bad idea. Super bad idea. The room spins and my body screams at me. I see that Ty is still next to me and lay back down.

"You heard it too?" Ty asks.

I squeeze my eyes shut. "Yeah, what was that?"

"I don't know. I'm going to go investigate." Ty gets out of bed, and the shift in the mattress causes me to groan, and I open my eyes to give him the evil eye. "Sorry, Allison. I'll get you some more pain medicine when I come back."

Ty/Grant is so cute in his sweatpants and T-shirt. You can see his muscles through the shirt, and his tousled brown hair with blonde tufts makes him look sexy. I haven't had time to process the fact that he's the one I've been flirting with for months. And that he's here...in my bed. But I digress. There could be a murderer or psycho killer in my apartment, and I can barely move. I hope Sexy Twin Guy can fight him off. I mean, he does look strong. I slowly roll to my side, thankful the bruise is on the other one and face the door with wide eyes, trying to listen for an altercation.

"All clear, but we're in trouble," Ty calls.

I gingerly sit up in bed. "Why? What's going on?"

"Hold on, I'll be right there."

Ty pads into my bedroom with medicine, fresh water, and…flowers.

"Where did you get those?"

"I think you had a delivery this morning, and I think it may have been Oliver." He gestures to the flowers.

"Are you sure they aren't from your mom?"

"No, I called her last night and told her what happened and let her know I was staying with you to watch you sleep. She wouldn't have been mad. She would have come in and cooed all over you. I tried to call Olly to tell him what happened so he could be here for you, but he wouldn't answer my calls. I guess we both fell asleep and I'm thinking," he raises his brows, "he may have found us in bed together."

"Oh no," I gasp. "What should we do?"

"I don't know, but I can tell you I'm pissed that he would think I would steal his girl. Although we did have a relationship before you met him." He winks.

"Yes, but…do you plan on telling me exactly what the deal is with your name and how, out of all the trainers in California, you end up being my neighbor?" He nods.

"Allow me to *formally* introduce myself. I'm Tyler Grant Hudson. My family calls me Ty and my clients call me Grant. Get it? Grant-it Fitness? It worked perfectly with my middle name, so I used it. I had no idea Oliver's Ally was my Allison. I mean, I know the name is the same, but I've only ever thought of you as Allison, and you are just as cute and beautiful as I thought you were. Your voice matches you perfectly." He kneels beside me and brushes his finger along my cheek. I melt.

"That makes a lot of sense… and thank you, but I can see why Oliver would be worried about losing me to you. You're a smooth talker. So let me be clear: I'm with Oliver and I wouldn't cheat on him," I confirm, backing away from his touch.

"I'm sure you wouldn't. And I would never do that to him either. I just didn't want our fun to end," he relents, and I sigh.

"We can still have fun. Our relationship has meant a lot to me. But what is between me and Oliver is different, and I refuse to do anything that would risk that. Okay?" I look up at him almost teary-eyed from both the lingering ache in my body and pain in my heart.

"Okay," he nods, "I understand. Plus, you obviously

make a cute couple," he smirks. I roll my eyes and my head sways, so I rest it back on my pillow. "Are you okay? Here, take some medicine. You might need to go to the hospital today."

"Nothing's broken, just extremely sore."

"I know, I'm just worried about your head." I groan.

"It's fine. I was just dizzy for a second. We need to go find Oliver, and if I somehow get worse, you can both take me to the hospital. Let me get dressed and we'll go." I rise out of bed, and thankfully, the dizziness is gone. Like I told Ty, I'm just sore.

I pad to the bathroom and check my reflection in the mirror. I'm covered in bruises, and my hair is smooshed up the back of my head creating a bushy halo of wayward strands. I'm stricken with horror knowing that Grant saw me like this and try to brush my hair down with my fingers only to nearly jump out of my skin when they skim over the goose egg in the middle of the halo. I groan, take a deep breath, and then wash my face with cool water. Once I've collected myself, I walk out to find Ellen sitting on my bed waiting for me. She's fresh-faced and dressed for the day in a trendy navy sweatshirt and jeans.

"Come here, honey. Let's get you dressed." She helps me out of Ty's shirt and hands me a button-down shirt so I don't have to pull anything over my head. Then she hands me a pair of jeans. She turns to give me some privacy. I let her know I'm done, and she turns back to me. I don't really need her help but my sore limbs are happy for the assistance.

"Would you be okay with me putting your hair up for you? That way it can be messy and loose so we won't have to brush over the big bump."

"That would be great." I close my eyes for a minute while she gently sweeps her fingers through my hair, soothing the pain as she does.

"Ty tells me you had an unexpected visitor this morning and he may have gotten the wrong idea," she tsks and shakes her head, "What am I going to do with that boy? He's always been jealous of his older brother." She secures my hair and steps back.

"Thank you, Ellen. I'm glad you're here. Do you have any words of advice?"

"Don't give up on him. He loves you and just couldn't bear to see you two together after the week he's had helping me. I'm sorry the house kept him away from you. I didn't know he was in a serious relationship until we talked after you helped me clean."

"We had just decided to take our relationship to boyfriend-girlfriend status when he disappeared. I had no idea what to think. Then Grant, I mean Ty, showed up and everything got messy."

"Well, now you can go clean it up. I know you two will work it out."

"Thanks."

"Ty! You can come back in here," Ellen calls.

"Hey, you look great. Ready to go?"

"Yeah. Time to go shake some sense into my boyfriend."

Ty walks me to Oliver's apartment and the cool breeze and sunlight are already making me feel alive again. I'm so thankful that the fall wasn't worse.

CHAPTER THIRTY-FOUR

Oliver

WHEN I RETURN to my apartment covered in sweat from running out my frustrations, I hop in the shower and get ready for the day. The doorbell rings as I'm getting out of the shower. I quickly throw on clothes and run to the door. Standing in front of me are a very angry-looking Ty and Ally. *Huh, I believe I should be the one who's mad.*

"May we come in," Ty asks. I concede and step back to let them in. Ally follows Ty and then takes a seat on the couch. I sit in the armchair across from them and look from one to the other.

Ty speaks first. "We were rudely awakened this morning by someone who was making assumptions and ran away like a baby before getting the whole story."

I balk. Ty holds up his hand.

"Stop right there. I don't want you saying a word until we say our peace. If you'll notice, your girlfriend has several bruises and one ginormous goose egg on the back of her head—that you can't see—from taking a spill down the stairs last night."

I take her in and wince at the true sight of her. "How did that happen?" I ask.

"Well, it seems that Ally put two-and-two together when she realized that I go by Grant at work."

"What?" I look between them again.

Ty continues. "It seems that your Ally is my Allison." I balk again and he realizes how that just sounded and corrects himself. "What I mean is, Ally is Allison Moore, she's the one who updates my websites."

"He's the liquid moo guy?" I ask Ally.

She nods.

"You called my shake liquid moo?" Ty asks her.

"This isn't the time," she says to Ty, patting his arm, and then looks back at me.

"Grant and I have been friends for five years. We've gotten close, but we would never betray your trust, and I would never cheat on you. I went over to see if *your brother* wanted to get some dinner last night, and when he answered a work call, I was taken off guard and fell down the stairs."

"The only reason I was in bed with her was to make sure she didn't have a concussion."

"Do you?" I ask with concern.

"No, I'm okay now. Just super sore."

"Oh good." I put my hand to my chest in relief. I

couldn't handle anything happening to her. "I guess I owe you both an apology for jumping to a very wrong conclusion and not trusting you."

"You do," Ty says and Ally nods along with him.

"I'm sorry." I get up and sit next to Ally on the couch, gently pulling her to my side.

"Thank you. I know we haven't known each other long, but I would never do that to you. I'd at least break up with you first before I started dating your brother." I let her go in a state of shock, but then she starts laughing. "Got ya."

"If you weren't hurt, I'd be tickling you senseless right now," I tease.

Ty clears his throat.

"I'm sorry too, man. I've been so upset being stuck at Mom's and not being able to get to Ally that when I saw you lying next to her, I just saw red."

"It's okay. I forgive you. Now, did someone mention there was a bar crawl coming up?" Ty asks, clapping his hands together.

"Are you going to be up for it," I ask Ally.

"I'd like to go. Do you think you could keep me company since I can't dance?"

"I think that could be arranged, *girlfriend*." I lightly bump her side, and she giggles.

"I like the sound of that."

"Me too."

"Well, now that you two are all lovey-dovey again. I'm going home and getting settled." He stands.

"Home. I like the sound of that, big brother," I say, standing with him and giving him a big hug. "Welcome back."

"Thanks," he says, pulling back and walking to the door.

"I assume you can get my good *friend,* Ally, home safe?"

"I definitely can. See ya later, man."

"Bye." Ally gives him a wave, and I join her back on the couch.

"I'm sorry for being an idiot."

"I'm just glad we worked it out. Apparently, it's good to communicate in an adult relationship. Speaking of communication, why didn't you call or email me about what was going on at your mom's?"

"I called and it went straight to voicemail, so I sent you a long email about the whole fiasco."

"What? No you didn't." She grabs her phone and checks her email. "See, nothing," she says, holding up her phone with her messages sorted by sender.

I grab my phone and quickly scroll through my sent folder. "Crap." I hang my head and show her my phone. Yes, the big, long email is there, but I forgot the *E* at the end of 'Moore,' so it didn't go through. "I'm so sorry." I look up at her with puppy dog eyes, seeking forgiveness.

"Let me see it." She reads the long, eloquent email I sent stating my undying love and need to be with her while all the things were keeping me away.

"I forgive you. But can you send it to me again? I'd like to frame the part where you call me an angel."

"I'd be happy to." I correct the address and resend, waiting for the notification tone to ring. Once the email is safely in her inbox, I place our phones on the coffee table. "Now, how about I kiss your bruises and make them all better." Ally giggles and I start with her lips.

"Those aren't bruised."

I laugh. "I know, but I couldn't resist. Now, let's get you in my bed so I can make you feel better." She laughs and lets me carry her to my room, where I gently lie her down and proceed to smother her with kisses.

CHAPTER THIRTY-FIVE
Allison

I STAYED AT Oliver's last night and we are now at my apartment getting ready for the bar hop. Nico was able to make me three more shirts for the boys and Ellen.

Morgan's on her way over to pregame before we meet the rest of the group at Loco Larry's.

Ty answers the door when Morgan knocks.

"Hey Oliver. Is Ally ready?" I hear Morgan ask.

"Hey Morgan, I'll be right out," I call from my bedroom as I'm knotting my t-shirt so it's a little more fitted but still covers most of my bruises.

When I come out with Oliver in tow, Morgan's eyes go wide with shock.

"Holy shit! You're…" She swivels and points to Oliver and then Ty.

"Ty. Nice to meet you," Ty supplies, shaking her hand.

"Ally, why didn't you tell me he was coming?" she asks.

"I thought I'd surprise you." I wink. "I did tell him he could come with us when he got here."

"Ally, could I see you in your bedroom for a moment?" She pushes me back in my room, and I hear the boys snicker. "How could you not tell me he was coming? He's freaking hot, and I'm in this ridiculous gray T-shirt with paint splotches on it. Where are your scissors?"

"In my middle bathroom drawer."

Morgan runs and grabs the scissors and quickly makes the shirt a V-neck crop top. "There, much better. How does my hair look?" Her pin straight hair is shiny and perfect with not a strand out of place.

"Morgan, you look hot as always. Now, let's go."

"Are you guys ready to go?" I ask as we come back out to the living room.

"We sure are," Ty cheers.

"Great. Let's go get your mom."

"What?!" Ty blurts out.

"Oh, oops. I may have invited your mom to come with us when I was helping clean your apartment." I coyly shrug.

"That's so not cool." Ty laughs.

"It will be fine. Just stick with Morgan, and your mom can dance with the other girls." Morgan glares at me. I give her the bestie eyeballs that say, *you know you want him, so I'm just making it happen.*

"I can get on board with that," Ty says, sidling up to Morgan. "Shall we?" He holds his arm out to her, and they link elbows and make their way to the door.

I look at Oliver and laugh.

"Mom," Ty gasps in surprise when he opens the door.

"Hi, Honey. You guys ready?" Ellen asks as she walks in.

"Are you seriously going with us tonight?" Ty asks her.

"Of course, I'm a single lady in the city. I can't wait to go dancing. I haven't been in so long." Ellen wiggles her hips in skinny jeans that are accompanied by a tight corset-style red shirt. "Cute shirt," she says to Morgan and we both laugh.

"Glad you like it because we have one for you," I inform her.

Seriously?" Ellen asks, holding it up.

"Come on, I'll show you how to make it work." Morgan leads her into my bedroom, and when they come out their shirts look the same. Ellen has killer abs. I might secretly hate her at the moment. "Oh, I almost forgot!" Morgan grabs her bag and pulls out some neon body paint. She adds splashes to Ellen, Ty, and Oliver, but when she gets to me, she stops. "Where did all these bruises come from?"

"I took a spill down the stairs."

"Oh my gosh. I'm so glad you're okay. How did you fall? Why was I not called?" Morgan rattles off while grasping my shoulders.

I point to Ty. "It's his fault. I overheard him answer a work call and found out he was Grant. I didn't call because he immediately scooped me up and took care of me."

"Wait. This is the Grant guy you told me about? The flirty client? That Grant?"

"Yes, that Grant." I laugh at her description and quickly look at Oliver to make sure he's okay, but he's laughing along with us.

"Then how is he also Ty?"

"Tyler Grant Hudson. I use my middle name for business," Ty interjects.

"Ah, wow. I did not see that coming." She looks at all of us stunned then quickly recovers and finishes painting over my bruises. As she's painting, she clears her throat and addresses the boys. "In the future, I would like to be notified if something happens to my girl."

"Yes ma'am," Ty and Oliver say in unison. We all laugh, and Morgan takes a step back to look at her artwork.

"Perfect! You look great. Let's go get our groove on." Morgan leads our tiny group out the door and down the street to Loco Larry's.

OLIVER AND I have been sitting most of the night, and we are finally back at Finnegan's and this time *we're* sitting in the quiet corner booth. What a difference a month makes. I'm so happy we worked everything out and he's here with me tonight. I'm not even ashamed to admit we've been having some pretty strong make-out sessions at each stop, but nothing tops the ones between Morgan and Ty. He hasn't left her side all night, and there has definitely been some dirty dancing going on. It's time for another round of beers, so Oliver and I move to the bar and order another round from Luke. I'm suddenly not so jealous of his boyfriend now that I have a hunky one of my own.

"Two more shots my good barkeep," Ty says as he and Morgan lean against the bar and start kissing.

"Oooh, if all this works out, I might finally get some grandbabies," Ellen cheers, walking up behind them and ordering a glass of white wine. I blush and Oliver groans. I don't think Ty and Morgan heard her at all.

When Oliver and I finish our beers, we sneak out of the bar and go back to my place.

"Well, it looks like Ty and Morgan hit it off," Oliver says as he undresses and gets into bed.

"They really have. Honestly, I think they are perfect for one another."

"How so?" Oliver asks.

"Well, they both have had trouble with long-term relationships and have a flirtier nature. Maybe they will mellow each other out," I add, gingerly pulling my hair up in a bun before washing my face.

"Maybe. I just hope he's not jumping into something too soon. He's only been here for a few days."

"I guess we'll see tomorrow, in the light of day," I say while rubbing in my moisturizer as I join him in bed.

"Let's not talk about them anymore. I'd much rather focus on us," Oliver says and pulls the cover over our heads.

After a round of euphoric bliss, my body no longer hurts, and I drift off to sleep.

I WAKE TO the morning light streaming in the window after only a few hours of sleep to find Oliver watching me.

"Good morning, boyfriend," I whisper.

"Good morning, girlfriend," he whispers back. "Would you like some breakfast?"

"I'd love some coffee and those Danish from Joe's you got after our first night together."

"I'm on it." Oliver jumps out of bed and throws on a sweatshirt with his joggers. "I'll be right back. Don't go anywhere."

"I won't. I love when you bring me breakfast in bed," I assure him.

"I know you do." He winks at me on his way out the door.

I sit and think about how lucky I am to have found Oliver. And Ty. I'm so glad we're all together in one city and can't wait to see what the future holds for us. Even though I like breakfast in bed, I pad out to the kitchen and pour myself a glass of orange juice while I wait.

Oliver returns with Ellen in tow.

"Look who I found out in the hall." Oliver puts the coffees and Danish down on the table in front of me.

"Ellen! How are you awake right now?" I ask in surprise. She's completely dressed, her hair is styled, and she's in full makeup.

"I didn't drink too much, but I had an absolute blast! I kept up better than those younger girls. You gotta learn how to pace yourself with the alcohol. Did you all not learn anything in college?" She laughs.

"Is Ty still asleep?"

"I'm not even sure if he's in his room. I was going to run for some breakfast when I found Oliver."

"Hm, I wonder if he's at Morgan's?" I say out loud.

"Maybe we shouldn't talk about this in front of my mom," Oliver suggests, and I quickly change the subject.

"So, tell us. Did you meet anyone?" I ask. "Inquiring minds want to know," I add, waggling my eyebrows.

"La la la. I don't want to hear this either," Oliver says, covering his ears.

"Actually, I did. But nothing serious, we just danced a lot."

"Whew. So, no stepdad material?" Oliver asks, removing his hands and plating the Danish.

"No, just some good old fun."

"What's he like?" I ask.

"He's tall, dark hair, dark eyes, muscular. And he has an accent. Latin, I think."

Oliver and I give each other a look.

"What's his name, Mom?"

"Daveed. Why?" she asks nonchalantly, picking up a pastry.

We both drop our Danish and yell, "Nooooo," in unison.

Stay tuned for more laughs with Ally, Oliver, Ty, Morgan, and Ellen, too, in Warm Up to Love.

www.ingramcontent.com/pod-product-compliance
Lightning Source LLC
Chambersburg PA
CBHW031526310726
48971CB00008B/2366